"It isn't a game ... older we get, th... shifters. By you... hunting deer, too... ... *~~~~ to neip yourself. You'll have to have blood. More and more each year. And by the time you're an adult, deer won't be enough. Nothing's going to satisfy you. Nothing except human blood."*

YEAR OF THE CAT

The terrifying new trilogy by Zoe Daniels

Book One: The Dream
When Holly Callison arrives at Los Gatos High School, she learns more than the legend of the panther. She unlocks the secret of her nightmares, the hunger in her soul—and the savage nature of her true self . . .

Book Two: The Hunt
As Holly explores the wild side of her secret destiny, she fears for the lives of the people she loves. But still, she cannot resist the power of the ancient rituals—and the bloodthirsty call of the hunt . . .

Book Three: The Amulet
(Available in August 1995)
In terror and desperation, Holly tries to cling to her human side. But the blood of the panther runs wild in her veins. And soon she's forced to choose sides—in the final war between predator and prey . . .

*This book also contains a special preview
of the exciting new thriller
by Leslie Rule:* Whispers From the Grave.

The YEAR OF THE CAT series by Zoe Daniels

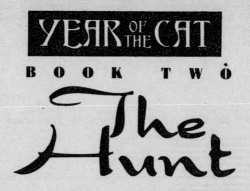

YEAR OF THE CAT
BOOK TWO
The Hunt

Zoe Daniels

BERKLEY BOOKS, NEW YORK

YEAR OF THE CAT: THE HUNT

A Berkley Book / published by arrangement with
the author

PRINTING HISTORY
Berkley edition / June 1995

ISBN: 0-425-14778-9

BERKLEY®
Berkley Books are published by The Berkley Publishing Group,
200 Madison Avenue, New York, New York 10016.
BERKLEY and the "B" design
are trademarks belonging to Berkley Publishing Corporation.

PRINTED IN THE UNITED STATES OF AMERICA

10 9 8 7 6 5 4 3 2 1

For Melinda Metz
who thought it would be fun
to write about the panthers.
She was right!

It was the same dream again.

Holly Callison flipped over in bed. Even though she was asleep, she knew what was happening.

It was the dream. All over again. A dream she hadn't had in . . . how long?

Holly could feel her brain frantically trying to answer the question, like when she took a test in biology class without studying the night before.

Her mind raced. Her heart beat fast. Her breathing was quick and jagged. How long had it been since she'd had the dream?

The answer came to her suddenly, as if someone had whispered it in her ear, and Holly felt herself relax against her pillow.

Panther Hollow.

That was it.

She hadn't had the dream since that night in Panther Hollow. The night she received the Gift.

Holly stretched her legs beneath her favorite rose-patterned sheets and tried to fall back into the kind of deep, dreamless sleep she had so many nights now. Still, something tickled at the edges of her mind. Something that wouldn't let her relax. If she hadn't had the dream in all these months, why now?

The question wouldn't go away. Holly tossed and turned. She had to figure out what was going on. It was important. She wasn't sure why, she only knew it was. She had to wake up.

But she couldn't.

The more she questioned the dream, the more it held her in its power, dragging her down one step at a time until she was surrounded by its sights and sensations. They crowded against her, close and hot, until she felt like all the air had been forced out of her lungs. She kicked her blankets. She swung her arms. She pushed against the images with her hands.

But still, they wouldn't go away.

She was in the school library. It was night. And no one had bothered to turn on the lights.

Holly looked around.

Just like before, the library was lit only by the eerie glow of the red exit signs above the doorways. Row after row of tall bookshelves filled the room and made it a maze of gray and black shadows.

She took a step forward, peering into the darkness. There was something there in the deeper shadows along the far wall. She could sense it.

Holly's fear vanished and she felt her lips lift into a slow, secret smile. Yes, there was something there. Just like the first time she had the dream.

But that time . . .

Holly got rid of the thought with a shake of her head that sent her curly red hair flying.

That time, she was afraid. Very afraid.

But not anymore.

Holly felt her spirits rise.

How could she be afraid now that she knew what was waiting in the shadows?

Without a second's hesitation, Holly hurried across the room. She found Alex Sarandon standing near the long, low cabinets that held the library's card catalogue. He was leaning back against the file drawers, his arms over his chest, his long legs out in front of him, crossed at the ankles. He was dressed all in black tonight and just the sight of him made Holly's heart start pounding all over again.

Alex's gorgeous face and irresistible charm had captured the hearts of just about every girl at Los Gatos High School. But Holly didn't care. They could daydream about Alex all they wanted, it didn't bother her a bit. He was hers—all hers—and she wasn't about to share him with anyone, not even Laila, his possessive twin sister.

Alex didn't look at Holly, but he must have sensed that she was there. He smiled and, stretching like a cat, he straightened his broad shoulders and lifted his chin. He moved away from the file cabinets, centering himself the way Holly had seen athletes focus, feet slightly apart, arms straight at his sides, head high. For one electrifying moment, his gaze met Holly's. The red light of the doorway signs glinted in his eyes like an unquenchable fire. Even though he didn't say a word, Holly knew what he wanted her to do.

She waited for him to take the lead. Even after all these months, Holly was amazed at how easy Alex made it look, astounded that something she would have thought of as impossible only a short time ago could be so natural and so very exciting.

One second he was Alex. Tall, gorgeous Alex. Junior class president. Co-captain of the LGH football team. The next second . . .

Holly felt a ball of emotion wedge in her throat at the same time she felt her blood race through her veins.

The next second Alex was a panther, a sleek, beautiful panther whose green eyes flashed and sparked, a panther whose powerful muscles rippled beneath fur as black as midnight.

Holly was beside him instantly. She didn't need to look down at herself to know she had changed, too. She could feel the transformation all the way through to her bones. She was smaller than Alex, but she was just as beautiful, her movements as graceful, her senses as heightened, her fur just as shiny and black.

Side by side, they stole out into the hallway, their passing no more than a wavering in the night, a deeper blackness in the inky shadows that filled the school.

They were in the first-floor hallway before Holly knew it, the way you sometimes move around in the blink of an eye in a dream. Holly recognized the main entrance of the school and the huge mural of the Los Gatos panther on the wall opposite the doors. That's when she noticed the lights were on in the newspaper office.

Instinctively, she stepped back into the shadows. In all the times she and Alex had explored Los Gatos at night in their panther shapes, they had never even come close to any humans. But the lights meant that someone was around. And that could mean trouble.

Holly's stomach knotted. Unsure what to do, she looked at Alex.

If the bright light that spilled into the hallway bothered him in any way, Alex didn't show it. He settled himself in the shadows, directly below the picture of the LGH panther, and his gaze moved casually from Holly to the open doorway of the office.

"Aren't you going to see who's in there?"

It was not a question really. Not as much as it was a suggestion.

Holly shook her head. *"No."* She used the Gift to send her thoughts directly into Alex's mind, just like he used it to communicate with her. *"I don't want to see anyone. I don't want anyone to see me. I—"*

"Are you ashamed of what you are?" Alex raised himself up, his eyes sparkling with flecks of fire. He wasn't mad at her. Holly was sure of that. But he was disturbed, upset that she would even think to deny the wonderful Gift they shared.

As quickly as she could, Holly tried to soothe him. *"Of course I'm not ashamed. I just don't know what to do. I mean . . . if I see someone . . . if they see me . . . I . . . What do I do? Do I run the other way? Or do I try to look fierce and hope the person runs first?"*

Alex was far more skilled at using the Gift than any of the other shape-shifters. He knew how to transmit emotions as well as words. If panthers could smile, Holly was sure Alex would be grinning from ear to ear. *"Go ahead,"* he urged, amusement coloring his thoughts. *"Go see what will happen."* He gave her a sidelong glance. *"Or are you afraid?"*

Holly looked at the open door of the newspaper office. She looked at Alex. Her heart sank.

He was obviously waiting for her to accept his challenge. And just as obviously, he wasn't about to take no for an answer.

Step by reluctant step, Holly crossed the corridor. Her padded paws were noiseless against the green-tiled floor. She stopped outside the door of the newspaper office and peered around the corner.

Jason Van Kirk was busy pecking at the keys of an old manual typewriter.

Jason.

Holly felt a sigh tremble through her body.

Jason was one of her first friends at LGH and the first boy here who had asked her out on a date. He was a sweetheart, a really terrific guy. Always thoughtful. Always funny. Always nice.

She hadn't spoken to him much lately, not since that day last fall when she found out she had the Gift and joined the pack with Alex and the other shape-shifters. She thought about Jason from time to time, and she knew he thought about her. He was always leaving cards and notes in her locker at school. But Alex had warned her again and again to keep her distance from humans, and as much as Holly hated to admit it, she knew that was good advice.

She'd already broken Jason's heart once by splitting up with him to date Alex. She couldn't bear the thought of how he'd feel if he knew that she was a shape-shifter.

Holly sat back and watched Jason pound away at the typewriter keys. He was probably trying to get his "Cat Calls" column for the newspaper done before deadline, Holly thought with a chuckle. Jason was famous for finishing up his column at the very last minute.

As if he could feel the brush of Holly's thoughts, Jason jiggled his shoulders and looked up. A rush of panic froze Holly in place. She couldn't let Jason see her! Not like this.

But it was too late.

Jason squinted into the shadows outside the doorway and his attractive face split with an enormous grin.

"Holly! What are you doing here in the middle of the night?"

Jason bounced out of his chair and crossed the room to stand in front of Holly. He was still smiling, looking down at her and smiling, and Holly felt her blood turn cold.

What's wrong with him?

The question echoed, unanswered, in Holly's head.

Why was he smiling? Why was he looking at her like she was still Holly Callison, red-haired, freckle-faced Holly Callison? Why wasn't he disgusted? Why wasn't he afraid? Why didn't he see the panther that sat right in front of him?

"I don't suppose you're here 'cause you heard I was working late on my column, are you?" Trying his best to act sophisticated, Jason quirked his eyebrows, but Holly couldn't help but notice that he was shuffling from foot to foot, the way he always did when he was nervous.

"I mean, you didn't come all the way over here just to see me?" Jason's blue eyes lit with excitement. "Did you? That sure would be great. It's been ages since we've been able to talk. Really talk. I mean, you've been so busy with ... Alex ... and ... gosh, Holly, I sure have missed you!"

"If he gets much closer, he'll discover your secret."

Where the warning came from, Holly didn't know. The words echoed in her head, and she knew they were true. She backed away a step.

"Since when are you shy?" Jason took a step forward, closing the distance between them. He still didn't see what she was. He was looking at her in the exact same way he'd looked at her the night of the homecoming dance when she'd worn her new green satin dress with the rhinestone buttons and the low-cut neckline.

"I'm not going to bite." Jason laughed nervously. "I just thought we could talk. I had a pizza with Tisha after school today. She says you've been avoiding her, too. I don't get it, Holly. She's your best friend. At least she used to be. Poor kid, she doesn't understand what's going on either."

"He's looking right at you. He must see what you are."

Again the voice came into Holly's head. She

glanced over her shoulder toward Alex. He was gone.

"If Jason finds out, he'll tell everyone in Los Gatos," the voice warned her. *"Everyone will know about the shape-shifters. You'll be in danger. Alex will be in danger. You can't let that happen."*

The voice was right. Holly knew it. She could feel a prickle of warning all along her back. She had to do something. Now. Before it was too late.

". . . so I was talking to Tisha's boyfriend, Zack." Holly had been so busy listening to the voice inside her head, she hadn't realized Jason was still talking. He chattered on, as friendly as ever. "Zack's the one who told me about you making the cheerleading squad for basketball. I was pretty surprised. I know Laila's got a lock on who gets in and who doesn't and I know Laila doesn't think much of you. At least, she never used to. But then, I figured I had to believe Zack 'cause he's on the team." Jason's face turned a bright shade of red. "Well, I guess you do know that. You're one of the cheerleaders. Anyway, I was telling him . . ."

Odd, Holly had never noticed how fair Jason's skin was. His blush faded and she could see the delicate network of blue veins just below the surface of his left cheek. There was one vein that led right down to the hollow at the base of his neck. Holly watched it pulse, each beat coursing life-giving blood through Jason's veins.

No!

It was impossible to use her human voice when she was in this form, but Holly screamed the word inside her head. She fought to turn her face away. She didn't want to see Jason. She didn't want to look at the throbbing vein at the base of his throat. She didn't want to think about how warm his blood was or how just the thought of it was making her sharp canine teeth tingle.

But the more she fought against it, the more hypnotized Holly was by the sight. As if a cloud had covered them, the overhead lights dimmed. Jason's face blurred in front of Holly's eyes. He was still talking, but his words sounded garbled. They echoed in the stillness of the school, like they came from miles and miles away. The floor rose and fell and Holly's head spun like it did every time she rode the Tilt-O-Whirl at the county fair.

Only that little vein stayed in focus, pulsing, throbbing, vibrating to the rhythm of Jason's heartbeat.

No!

Holly tried to scream the word again. But even though her mind shrieked its refusal, she couldn't stop the reflex actions of her body. It was nature. It was instinct. And she couldn't help herself.

She took a step forward.

". . . so Zack says he's seen you do some really incredible stuff . . . cartwheels and flips . . . all those great gymnastics moves . . . I said to him that I knew you were a runner . . . your old school in Cleveland . . . never said anything about gymnastics . . . didn't that just figure . . . you'd be good at whatever you tried . . ." Jason's voice faded in and out.

Holly felt the powerful muscles of her back legs

tense, like springs coiled and ready to snap. Her nostrils flared with the scent of the inexpensive aftershave Jason slapped on after gym class. Her mouth watered.

For one moment she had a clear vision of Jason's eyes. They were sparkling down at her, blue as a spring sky, bright as a May morning. The next second the image faded and she was looking at his neck again. At the tiny, pulsing vein.

It was too much.

Holly propelled herself into the air.

It was only then that Jason saw her for what she was. In that one split second, Holly saw his face go pale, his mouth fall open. He didn't look afraid. He looked like someone had just destroyed everything he thought was right and good in the world.

No!

Holly fought against the uncontrollable impulse that made her knock Jason back against the nearest drawing table and bare her fangs.

No!

The word reverberated through her mind. It twisted through her soul.

No! No! No!

2

"No!"

Holly bolted up in bed. She was soaked with sweat. Her face was wet with tears. Her hair clung to her forehead and cheeks like long, snaky threads of sea-weed. With trembling fingers, she scraped the hair out of her eyes.

It was still dark.

There was a streetlight in front of the house two doors away and, hoping to make her heart slow down and her head stop pounding, Holly stared up at the blotchy patterns the light made on her ceiling. She drew in a long, painful breath.

A thought struck Holly suddenly and made her stomach go cold. She remembered the night she dreamed that she killed Mr. Tollifson, her biology teacher. She remembered how she woke up the next morning and found her clothes and shoes spattered with the mud of Harper's Mountain, where Mr. Tollifson's body was found.

Gingerly, Holly shifted beneath her blankets, checking to see if there was anything at the foot of her bed, anything like soiled clothing.

There wasn't.

She peered over the edge of the bed.

There was nothing on the floor, either.
Holly slumped back against her pillow.
It was a dream. Nothing but a dream.

> *Roses are red.*
> *Violets are blue.*
> *Won't you be in the play*
> *I've written for you?*

Don't miss your chance to be a part of the best play in LGH history—Dracula Meets the Los Gatos Panther by (Ta-da!) Yours Truly. Tryouts are today after school. Lots of juicy parts left (no pun intended).

P.S. Give it a try, you've got an ''in'' with the playwright! I can practically guarantee you a part.

Holly instantly recognized Jason's handwriting on the note she found taped to her locker. She should by now. He'd probably sent her at least a hundred notes since they'd broken up last fall.

But why did he have to write her one today?

In spite of the warmth of the heavy cable-knit sweater she was wearing, Holly shivered. The memory of the dream she'd had last night was still too fresh in her mind.

All she could picture was Jason's face the way it had looked when he found out she was a shape-shifter, when he realized that she was dangerous. All she could think of was the feel of his weight beneath her body. The smell of his fear. The taste of his flesh.

"What's that?"

It used to be that Alex could sneak up behind Holly and surprise her all the time. That wasn't true anymore. Her senses were too keen. But this time he caught her with her mind a million miles away. He wrapped his arms around her waist and rested his chin on her shoulder, and she jumped and let out a squeal.

Before Alex could see the note from Jason, Holly crumpled it and shoved it in her pocket. She pulled away from Alex and whirled around, but she couldn't quite look him in the eye. Not when she knew she was about to lie to him. She studied her shoelaces. "It's nothing," she said, at the same time she wondered why an innocent invitation to try out for the school play made her feel so guilty.

"Just a note. From . . . from Tisha," Holly decided at the last second. It was as good a lie as any and it sounded logical. Recovering her composure, Holly looked up at Alex and gave him the sweetest smile she could manage. "She wants to know if we can get together after school."

Like he did every day before biology, Alex grabbed Holly's books from her and set them on top of his stack. He headed toward the biology lab. "Are you going to go?"

Holly gave him a questioning look. "You said—"

"I said it wasn't safe to be around humans." Alex kept his voice down so no one else in the hallway could hear. He cast a glance at the other kids hurrying to their classes and his top lip curled like he just tasted something sour.

"They ask too many questions and they trigger emotions we sometimes can't control. But I don't see what difference a visit with Tisha would make. Do you? She's such a little thing. And so naive. I don't think it would hurt you to spend some time with her."

Holly shrugged to hide her confusion. Ever since that day last fall when she was officially initiated into the pack, Alex had been warning her to stay as far away from humans as she could. It was too risky, he told her. And she believed him.

She had stopped seeing Jason altogether and she only talked to Tisha once in a while. Her friends were Alex's friends now, and they were all shape-shifters: Tom and Raymond, Lindsey and Amber. And Laila, of course.

Holly felt a tiny thread of some uncomfortable emotion curl around her heart. It felt like loneliness and it hurt. She tried to push the thought out of her mind, but it just wouldn't go away. No matter how hard Alex tried to get her to be friends with the other shape-shifters, it just never seemed to work. There was a wall between them, Holly realized, and no matter what she did it was impossible to break it down.

There was always something there. Something that made them glance at each other knowingly when they thought Holly wasn't watching. Some secret she felt they still hadn't shared.

She would never be able to be friends with them.

Not really. Not the way friends are supposed to be friends.

Holly knew it in her heart.

They'd never be real friends the way Tisha was.

Before she could stop herself, Holly was thinking how nice it would be to get together with Tisha and talk girl talk over a large pizza and a couple pitchers of Coke. She missed Tisha and all the fun they'd shared.

The more she thought about it, the better the idea sounded. Holly still sat next to Tisha in biology. Maybe she could pass her a note? Maybe they really could get together today? Before they got as far as the biology lab, Holly was smiling.

Outside the lab room door, Alex handed Holly's books back to her. "No, I don't think seeing Tisha would hurt a bit," he said. "But it can't be today."

Holly felt her excitement melt like an ice cube in the hot July sunshine. "Why not?" she asked, trying hard not to sound too touchy and ending up sounding crankier than ever. "Why not today?"

Alex looked down at the pocket where Holly had stashed the note from Jason. Like moonlight sparking off cold, hard steel, his eyes gleamed and he smiled a smile that made Holly wince.

"Tryouts for the play are right after school," he said. His expression was suddenly as good-natured as his voice. Holly wondered if she hadn't imagined the cold glint of steel in his eyes.

"You're going, aren't you?" Alex turned up his smile a notch. "You should. I hear you've been invited specially by the author.'' Without another word, he went into the classroom and slid into his desk.

Holly didn't move. She couldn't. She stood in the hallway, frozen with astonishment. Automatically, she stuffed her hand into her pocket. The note was still there, tucked safely where she'd put it.

The thought, along with the class bell, jarred Holly back to reality. She bolted into the classroom like she'd been shot from a cannon.

Just as she was walking by Alex's desk, he grabbed her hand and smiled up at her. The sunlight that streamed in through the lab windows touched the edges of his teeth. ''I'm planning on trying out for the play, too.'' Alex threw back his head and laughed. ''Dracula! It's the perfect part for me, don't you think?''

Holly didn't answer. What was there to say? She pulled her hand away and hurried over to her desk. She dropped into her seat just as Mr. Carlton came into the room.

Mr. Carlton was the biology teacher who'd been hired to take over the class after Mr. Tollifson was killed. He was as tall and skinny as Mr. Tollifson had been short and round. He had a high, twangy voice that sounded like he was talking with a clothespin on his nose. It didn't help his class much. Mr. Carlton was one of the most boring teachers Holly had ever had. He told them to open their books to Chapter Twelve and started reading the book, word for word.

Holly groaned under her breath. She propped her elbows on the desktop and cradled her chin in her hands. Mr. Carlton was so busy reading, he wasn't looking at the class at all, and Holly took the opportunity to glance at Tisha.

After a couple seconds, Tisha looked up and gave Holly a quick smile, the kind strangers give each other when they pass on the street.

The look nearly broke Holly's heart. "Want to grab a pizza after play tryouts?" she whispered.

Tisha looked surprised. She poked her chin toward the other side of the room. "What about Alex?"

"What about him?" Holly tried her best to sound grown-up. "He won't mind. Besides, he doesn't own me."

"Doesn't he?" Tisha must have surprised even herself. She looked away. Biting her lower lip with her top teeth, she turned the page in her biology book, straightened the pens on the desk, and fumbled with her notebook. Finally, she turned back to Holly but she didn't look at her. "I can't today," Tisha said and Holly couldn't tell if she sounded disappointed or if she was just looking for an excuse. "Or tomorrow. Grammy needs my help at the store."

"Oh." There wasn't much more Holly could say. Suddenly she felt very alone. She flipped the pages in her book until she caught up to where Mr. Carlton was reading. She stared down at the pages and her eyes filled with tears. The words flowed together in front of her and Mr. Carlton's voice droned on and on in her ears.

"Thursday?"

Startled, Holly looked over at Tisha.

She fidgeted in her seat, as self-conscious as Holly. But in the split-second she lifted her eyes to meet Holly's, Tisha's face broke into the kind of open, friendly smile Holly remembered.

A warm feeling filled Holly and she felt her spirits lift. "Thursday," she said. "Gino's at four?"

Tisha didn't say another word. She just nodded and they both went back to following along as Mr. Carlton read Chapter Twelve.

When the bell rang, Holly took her time getting her things together. She knew Alex had to leave biology in a hurry to make it to his calculus class on time. It was way over in the Annex, a separate building that had been added to the back of the school when enrollment boomed a few years earlier. Holly had no place to go but a study hall. She could afford to take her time.

Holly propped her books in her arm and headed for the door. She was almost there when she heard someone call her name.

"Holly?" It was Jason's voice.

Holly didn't turn around. With the memory of last night's dream still so fresh in her mind, she was pretty sure she didn't want to talk to Jason. Not today.

"Holly?" He called her again.

It would be just plain rude to ignore him. Holly rolled her eyes. She turned around.

"Oh, hi, Jason. I didn't see you there."

"Yeah." Jason stared down at the worn toes of his sneakers. He looked up at Holly through the shock of blond hair that always seemed to be drooping over his forehead. "Did you get the note I left you? The one about play tryouts?"

"I'm not much of an actress." Holly knew that for sure. If she was, maybe she could actually carry on a conversation with Jason without feeling like a total creep. "I don't think being in a play is my style, I—"

"It's a great play." A shimmer of excitement sparkled in Jason's blue eyes. "Kind of a semi-romantic, artsy comedy-classic with overtones of Zen philosophy and scenes of out-and-out horror. If you know what I mean." He smiled a kind of half-embarrassed, half-proud smile that made him look as huggable as a teddy bear.

Holly couldn't help but smile back. "No," she admitted honestly. "I have no idea what you mean. But I'm sure the play will be great. Everything you write is. Like the program you did for the homecoming bonfire."

Holly regretted the words instantly. She'd gone to the homecoming festivities with Jason last fall. Neither one of them needed to be reminded about that.

"Yeah . . . well . . ." Jason shuffled his feet. "So anyway, this part. It's the best one in the play. Honest! It's not very big." Jason rolled his eyes.

"I guess that's not a great way to convince you, is it? What I mean is, I knew Laila would get Camilla's part even before I wrote the play. She always gets the lead, so I made sure it fit her to a T. She's going to play a sort of conceited snob who—"

Jason caught himself. "Sorry," he said. "I know

she's one of your friends now. Anyway, the part I had in mind for you is smaller. The character's name is Nancy. She's a servant in Dracula's house of horror. She's sweet. Kind of romantic. I wrote the part just for you.'' Jason blushed. He cleared his throat and launched into the rest of his sales pitch before Holly had time to object.

"It's not like you'll have a lot of lines to memorize or anything. That'll give us plenty of time to spend together . . .'' Holly thought it was impossible for Jason to look any more embarrassed. She was wrong. He turned fire-engine red all the way from his dimpled chin to the roots of his hair. He obviously hadn't meant to reveal that much of his plan. He changed the subject as fast as he could. "Alex told me he's trying out for the lead. With all those dark, mysterious good looks of his, he'll make a great Dracula.''

Jason had no idea how right he was. "Yeah, he will.'' It was all Holly could say.

"So you'll try out?'' Jason blurted out the question.

Holly didn't have the heart to disappoint him. "Maybe,'' she said. She moved toward the door.

But it was clear Jason wasn't finished yet. He didn't even try to follow her. He stayed right where he was and shifted the load of books he was carrying from his right arm into his left. "You know, I didn't say it in my note, but there's something else I'd like to talk to you about. I mean, sometime, when you have time and you're not busy and . . .''

Jason's voice sounded strange. He shrugged like it was no big deal, but Holly could tell something was bothering him. His eyes had lost their sparkle and he didn't look at all embarrassed or self-conscious now. He looked worried.

"It's just . . . well . . . well, it's something I just can't forget," Jason said. "I've tried. I spent all morning telling myself that it's nothing to get upset about. But I just can't seem to let it go." He dragged in a long breath and let it out again. "I had the weirdest dream about you last night, Holly."

Holly opened her mouth to answer him. But she couldn't. Her mouth was as dry as a desert. Her tongue was like sandpaper. Her heart was thumping so hard against her ribs, each beat made her feel like she was going to explode.

"A dream?" Holly tried to banish her terror with a giggle. It came out sounding more like a croak. "What sort of dream?"

Jason scrubbed his fingers through his hair. "That's just it. That's the part that's got me all confused. It was a good dream. I think." His face screwed up as if he was thinking very hard. "I mean you were in it. You and me. We were talking. In the newspaper office and—"

Jason's words stopped suddenly, like they'd been snipped with scissors. He leaned nearer and, placing one hand on Holly's arm, he stared into her face. "You look green," he said. "Is something wrong?"

"No. No, nothing's wrong. I'm fine." Holly stood rooted to the spot.

"You don't look fine." Jason shook his head. "But then, I'm not sure you were fine in the dream, either, and that's what's got me worried. We were talking. Just talking. But then you were all over me!" Jason let out a short bark of laughter. "Not that I'm complaining. Talk about a dream come true! I mean . . . gosh!" He made a sound halfway between a whistle and a moan. "But the thing that's got me worried is that, in the dream, you were Holly. But you weren't." The expression on Jason's face softened and his hand tightened around Holly's arm. She could feel his warmth and concern, even through her heavy sweater. "I know that doesn't make any sense," he said. "And I know I shouldn't be bothering you with it, but—"

"You're right. It doesn't make any sense." As fast as she could, Holly shook off Jason's hand. She didn't want to hear what he had to say. She didn't want to think about it. She wanted to get away from here, to get away from him as fast as she could.

"It was just a dream," she said, moving to the door. Her voice was high and tight with fear. "Just a dream, do you understand? I'm Holly. Just Holly. And I was never talking to you in the newspaper office. Not in your dream. Not ever."

"Okay. Okay." Both hands held up in surrender, Jason backed off. "You don't have to get so crazy about it. It was just a dream. I told you that. I knew it from the start." Dazed by her reaction, Jason massaged the back of his neck with one hand.

"I knew it was a dream," he said, almost to himself. "It had to be, the way you were dressed."

His words hung in the silence between them. They echoed in Holly's ears, burned in her chest. She ran her tongue over her lips and squeezed her eyes shut as if she could hide from Jason's words.

"What was I wearing?" she asked.

"Well, that was the funny thing." Jason's voice was thoughtful. "You usually dress in blues and greens. They go with your red hair best and you always look great. But in the dream . . . Holly, in the dream you were dressed all in black."

3

"Listen to this." Alex was sitting on the top step of the gazebo that stood smack in the center of the Los Gatos town square. He tipped the papers in his hand toward the single lightbulb that hung high up in the open rafters, cleared his throat, and started to read.

" 'Dracula sweeps across the room and stands in front of Nancy. She is weak with fear, helpless with desire. Drac has bigger fish to fry. He is after the mysterious and enchanting Camilla. Nancy is nothing to him. He hurries by her and just the power of his passing causes Nancy to faint.' "

Alex burst into a laugh that vibrated through the frosty air. "That Jason! It's the only scene we have together in this whole play and he makes it so innocent it hurts! Dracula sucks the blood out of every other girl in the play. But not Nancy! He just walks by Nancy and she's out like a light. What a guy Jason is, protecting your honor to the last! Tell me, Holly, is that why you think he's so great? Holly? Holly?"

"Huh?" Holly's head snapped up. She'd been listening to Alex. She was sure she had. But somewhere between when he started reading from his script and when he'd called her name, she got lost. She was certain she heard every word he said. But none of it made sense. It was like he was talking another language. One she didn't understand.

Hoping to get rid of the cobwebs that clouded her thinking, Holly shook her head. How could she possibly pay attention to anything Alex was saying, she asked herself, when she was so worried about Jason?

Tucking the thought away where she hoped Alex wouldn't discover it, Holly spun to face him. "Sorry." She gave him a tight smile. "I guess I wasn't listening."

"That's pretty obvious." Alex tossed his script down on the floor of the gazebo. In one graceful motion, he got up and went over to where Holly was standing. He rested his hands against the railing, one arm on either side of her. The look in his eyes warmed the air between them.

"You haven't been listening to a thing I've said all night," Alex told her. "Your body's here. But your brain's a couple light years away. What's wrong?"

Wrong? How could she possibly tell him what was wrong when he was looking at her this way?

Hoping to calm the tremor of excitement that quivered through her every time Alex was near, Holly focused on the time and temperature sign that flashed in front of the bank across the park.

11:43 P.M.

31 degrees.

She watched the yellow numbers wink at her through the frigid air.

11:44 P.M.

31 degrees.

Holly shivered inside her heavy winter jacket. It wasn't that she was cold. It was a lot colder in Cleveland this time of year.

It was just that the memory of her latest dream wouldn't leave her alone. It was with her all through school today, all through play tryouts after school. It wouldn't go away. Not even now when all she wanted to do was enjoy Alex's company.

Holly forced her gaze back to Alex. Like it or not, they had to talk about it—before Alex had the chance to think there was something *really* wrong. Before she went to bed tonight, and risked dreaming about Jason again.

Alex caught her looking at him and a small, concerned smile danced around his mouth. "I asked what was wrong." He moved a step closer, so close, Holly could feel the heat of his body, even through her coat. She couldn't look away now, not even if she wanted to. His green eyes held hers with a hypnotic look that made it clear she had to tell him. She had to tell him everything.

"Remember last fall?" Holly tried to begin at the beginning, even though she was afraid that would make the explanation hopelessly long and boring. "Last fall, when I first started dreaming about the panther? I mean, I thought it was a dream. But it wasn't, right? What I mean is, you were summoning me. I wasn't dreaming at all. You were calling me in my sleep. Right?"

"That's right." With one finger, Alex traced the outline of Holly's jaw, from her left ear, over her chin, up to her right ear. He tucked a curl of hair behind her ear and flicked his thumb and forefinger over the dangling black earrings he'd given her for Christmas.

"I wanted to be with you," he said. "So I summoned you. Of course, that was before I knew you were the One. That you were a shape-shifter. That was before I knew we could be together for real, with nothing ever getting between us."

It would have been easy to surrender to the incredible feel of Alex's hand against her skin. It would have been easy to talk herself into forgetting Jason altogether. Too easy. Holly charged on before the heat of Alex's touch melted her determination completely. "Could Laila do anything like that?" she asked.

Alex took a step back. "What are you saying? That Laila's been messing with your dreams?"

Holly pushed away from the railing. She hurried across the gazebo and stood as far away from Alex as she could, hoping the distance and the cold would force her to think more clearly. "I know it sounds bizarre. But I guess that is what I'm saying. I had this dream, you see, and—"

"It's not possible."

Alex slashed one hand through the air, scattering every bit of her argument. "I summoned you in those dreams, Holly. Me." He stabbed his thumb at his chest. "Laila was able to tap into what I was doing, but she isn't capable of doing that kind of thing on her own. No." He snorted. "I take it back. She's capable, all right. But she's lazy. Too lazy to practice using the Gift in all the ways it can be used. She couldn't have tampered with your dreams without me knowing it. She doesn't have the skill.''

He was right, of course, and Holly was glad. She wanted Alex to be right. She wanted him to chase away her troubles as easily as he'd destroyed her argument—with one swipe of his arm.

Only if Alex was right, how did Jason pop into her dream last night? And how was Jason able to share the same dream?

The question nagged at the back of Holly's mind. She couldn't let it go. Not that easily.

Dreading what she knew she had to do, Holly went back to stand in front of Alex. She looked up at him. Something in his expression told her she should drop the subject right here and now. But she couldn't. Not yet. Not until she had some answers. ''If all that is true, then tell me how two people can have the same dream,'' Holly asked. ''The exact same dream. Tell me how that can happen, Alex.''

''The same dream.'' He rolled the words over his tongue like they were some new food he'd never tried before, a food he wasn't sure he liked. ''Are you sure?''

''Of course I'm sure.'' Holly stuffed her hands into her pockets. ''And I don't get it. I tried to figure it out on my own, but I just don't know enough about the Gift, about all the things we're able to do. That's why I suspected Laila. I—''

''Who is it you're dreaming about?''

Faced with the question point-blank, Holly knew she didn't dare lie about the answer, as much as she would've liked to. "Jason," she said, her voice barely louder than a whisper.

Alex tilted his head as if he didn't hear. "Who?"

"Jason," she said again, this time so loud that it echoed against the rafters. "I had a dream about Jason. Last night. Kind of like the dream I had the night Mr. Tollifson was killed."

Holly could've kicked herself the moment the words were out of her mouth. When Holly learned about the panthers, Alex told her all about what happened to Mr. Tollifson. How in her panther shape, she blundered into Mr. Tollifson's animal trap. How Alex was forced to kill Mr. Tollifson to save her. Alex was terribly upset by the whole thing and Holly promised she would never mention it again. Now here she was, practically yelling it for the whole town to hear.

In spite of the frosty air, Holly felt her cheeks get hot. She lowered her voice and got back on track as fast as she could. "Jason . . . He told me he had the same dream about me last night."

Alex's eyes were suddenly as cold as the night. "I didn't realize you two were still that friendly," he snapped back at her.

"Oh, get real!" Holly looked up at the dangling lightbulb, fighting against the anger that threatened to send her up in flames. This was supposed to be a logical discussion. It had turned into an out-and-out accusation. She wasn't sure how. She only knew that the look in Alex's eyes said everything he wouldn't say out loud. He thought she was seeing Jason again.

Before Holly could deny it, Alex went over to

where he'd left his script. He bent down and picked it up. "I wondered about this." He weighed the stack of papers in his hands.

"I wondered how Jason could write a play that was so accurate. Have you read it yet?" He waved the script under Holly's nose. "I play Dracula. Laila plays Camilla, the leading lady in Dracula's life. But in this version, Dracula and Camilla live here in Los Gatos. They're also shape-shifters. You know, typical vampire stuff. They change into bats, wolves. The usual. But good ol' Jason, he's also incorporated bits and pieces of the Los Gatos legend into the whole thing. At the very end of the play, Dracula turns into a panther. He disappears into the woods on Harper's Mountain."

Holly stared at him in amazement, almost afraid to ask if he was saying what she thought he was saying. Before she could force the words out of her mouth, Alex spun around. The gazebo was big enough to hold the high school band, but he covered the length of it in four lightning-quick strides. He turned at the far side and came back to stand in front of Holly, each of his steps as graceful as a cat's, each look he gave her cold enough to chill her soul.

"That's not where the similarities end." Alex's voice was far more controlled than the fire she saw burning deep inside his eyes. "Dracula and Camilla share their special gift with five other characters in the play. They kill one person in the first act. A teacher."

"And you think . . . ?" The words caught in Holly's throat. She tried again. "Are you saying that you think Jason was able to write the script because I told him about you? That I told him about the shape-shifters?"

"I'm saying that there are a number of remarkable coincidences in this play." Alex tossed the script down. It landed on the wooden floor with a loud smack. "I'm saying that your friend Jason seems to know an awful lot of stuff he shouldn't know. Stuff he has no business knowing. I'm saying that there's only one person who could have told him those things."

As piercing as the cold, Alex's words hung on the frosty air. Holly wrapped her arms around herself, trying to keep out the chill. She looked down at the script that lay on the floor between them. She looked up at Alex. She wasn't sure what hurt more, the look on Alex's face or the sting of his accusation.

"I would never betray you." Holly's words escaped on the end of a sob. "You know I would never do that. I couldn't. I wouldn't. I—"

"Then explain it to me." His hands out to her, Alex took one step forward. He stopped himself a full five feet away and Holly could tell that he had to fight to keep from getting any nearer. He wanted to come to her. She could tell that from the agonized look on his face. He wanted to hold her in his arms. But he needed the truth first.

Holly gave it to him. "You said it yourself, a remarkable string of coincidences. The Dracula story is world famous. It's not unusual that Jason would use it, especially with his sort of warped sense of humor. The Los Gatos panther story's a natural, too. He wrote all that stuff for homecoming, didn't he? All that stuff about the legend? He's just using it again. That's all.''

''And the rest of it?''

Holly lifted her shoulders. ''Luck. Coincidence. Call it whatever you want. You'll never be sure. There's only one thing you can be sure of. I never told Jason a thing. I never will. I haven't talked to Jason in months. Not really. Not for more than a couple minutes.'' Holly tried her best to sound brave, but she couldn't keep up the act for long. Her lower lip started to quiver. Her eyes filled with tears. ''How could you even think I would do a thing like that? How could you doubt me?''

Before she had a chance to say more, Alex hurried to her. He wrapped his arms around Holly and pressed her close to his heart. He nuzzled his cheek against her hair. ''I don't doubt you. I swear I don't. I just . . . I just want to keep you safe, Holly. I just want to be sure our secret doesn't get into the wrong hands. Do you have any idea what would happen if it did?''

Holly ran the back of her hand over her cheeks and looked up at Alex. ''No. I don't know what would happen. I don't want to know. Not now. Maybe not ever. But you have to believe me, Alex. I would never tell . . . never tell . . .''

This time she couldn't stop her tears. Alex smiled down at her. He wrapped one arm around her shoulders and led her over to the steps. He sat down and pulled Holly down beside him, his arm still around her.

"I'm sorry," he said. "I didn't mean to make you cry. Maybe you're right. Maybe it is all just a coincidence. I'm sorry I got so worked up about it. You've got to see it from my point of view. Whether I like it or not, I'm responsible for all the other shape-shifters. They don't understand the power inside them. Not yet. They don't know how to use it. Someone has to watch over them until they're mature enough to take responsibility for themselves. There isn't anyone else but me. I feel I have to take charge. I don't want anything to happen to any of them." He kissed the tip of Holly's nose. "I don't want anything to happen to you."

Holly sighed, letting go of all the misery inside her. This was all she wanted—all she had ever wanted—to be in Alex's arms. It was enough for now. It was enough for always. She settled her head against Alex's shoulder and closed her eyes, enjoying the feeling.

"You know, I do have to own up to something."

Alex's voice, soft and low in her ear, lured Holly out of her daydream.

He looked at her sheepishly and Holly wondered if it was a trick of the light, or if he really was blushing.

"It's not just you I'm concerned about," Alex confessed. "I know you well enough to know you can take pretty good care of yourself. It's not you that's got me worried. It's Jason."

"Jason?" Holly couldn't have been more surprised. She puckered her lips and wrinkled her nose. She gave Alex a kind of disbelieving half-smile. "You're worried about Jason? Why?"

Alex drew in a long breath and looked up at the

ceiling. He seemed to be deciding just what to tell her. "Let me explain it this way." Without another moment's hesitation he scooped Holly into his arms and kissed her. Hard.

"Alex!" Holly tried to wriggle away. It wasn't that she didn't like what he was doing, it just seemed like an awfully public place to do it.

But no matter how hard she tried to pull away, Alex wouldn't let her.

After the first kiss, Holly's determination turned to Silly Putty. After the second one, she was way past caring where they were or who saw them.

All she knew was that she was here. In Alex's arms. And the taste of his mouth was warm and inviting. And the touch of his hands made her head spin.

Holly tipped her head back, giving Alex the opportunity to deepen the kiss.

But even that didn't seem to be enough for him.

He pressed Holly closer and slid his hands from her back to her neck. He massaged the sensitive skin along her jawline and trailed his hands along her shoulders.

A rush of panic set Holly's heart pounding. Or maybe it was just the feel of Alex's lips on hers that made her feel like she was about to burst.

She wasn't sure.

She wasn't sure of anything anymore, except that everywhere Alex touched, everywhere he kissed her, her skin felt like it was on fire. Pretty soon she'd go up in flames. She was sure of that, too.

And she didn't care about that, either.

Holly wrapped her arms around Alex's neck, her fingers spreading through the fringe of dark hair that tumbled over his collar.

That's when she felt the change start to happen.

The ends of Holly's fingers tingled. The skin on her arms prickled. Her veins surged with power.

"I'm changing." Holly pushed away from Alex. "I'm changing. Here. Now." She looked down at her hands. They weren't hands at all anymore, they were paws. As Holly watched, her pink, polished nails grew longer, until each one was a razor-sharp claw. She turned panic-stricken eyes on Alex and what was left of her human voice rose up into the frigid night air like the last cry of a lost soul. "I've never changed like this before. Not without warning. Not without your help. Alex! Help me! I can't stop it and it hurts." She clutched her stomach. "It hurts like it did that first night up on Harper's Mountain."

The town square began to spin in front of Holly's eyes, slowly at first, then faster and faster until she couldn't tell buildings from trees, trees from streetlights. They all melted together into one smear of light, a light so bright it stabbed Holly right behind her eyes and made her cry out for help.

It was over as fast as it started.

Everything stopped spinning and Holly found herself on her hands and knees on the floor of the gazebo. She rested her forehead against the worn floorboards and sucked in a couple lungfuls of cold air.

Breathing hurt. So did moving.

Holly slumped on her side and lay there, listening

to the frantic, furious beating of her heart.

In a couple seconds Alex stepped into her line of sight. He knelt beside Holly and gently smoothed away the hair that had fallen in front of her eyes. "I wish there was another way we could have done that. I'm sorry. There wasn't. You had to find out. Sooner or later. You had to know."

"Know what?" Holly struggled to sit up. Her head was pounding like a whole herd of elephants was in there jumping rope. Dropping back to the floor, she closed her eyes and listened to Alex's explanation.

"Don't you remember?" he asked. "When you first learned you had the Gift. I told you that emotions are hard to control. I told you sometimes we can't help what happens when we're very angry, or very excited, or feeling very passionate."

Holly made herself open her eyes. She wanted to watch Alex's face when she questioned him. "And that's what happened?"

"That's what happened. I took you too far. Further than you should have been taken before you've mastered the Gift."

"On purpose?" Holly forced herself to sit up. At least her head had stopped spinning. Now everything just looked a little pale, like she was watching the world through a TV set that needed a color adjustment. "You did that to me on purpose?"

Alex made an impatient gesture. "That's the point. Don't you see? You did it to yourself. And you didn't even know it. And once you knew it, there was no way you could stop it." He sat back on his heels, his voice calm and even, like he was discussing the big play of last weekend's basketball game.

"You had to find out what it was like, Holly. You had to find out that you can change anytime. Anytime. Anyplace. Take one shape-shifter, add a healthy dose of passion and bingo! Panther!" Alex smiled a smile that was completely without humor. "Do you see what I'm getting at? If you're with a human, it could be dangerous. Not so much to you, but to the human. It could be fatal to the human."

Holly bounded to her feet and clamped her hands over her ears. She didn't want to hear it. She didn't want to hear any of it.

Her legs were still wobbly and her stomach was doing flip-flops, but Holly managed to brace herself against one of the carved columns that held up the ornate roof. She propped her hands on her knees and fought to regain her self-control. Alex was watching her. Just watching her. And something about the clinical way he was looking at her, something about the detached way he'd explained the whole thing, filled her with defiance.

"Then tell me how you're able to get away with it?" she asked with a sarcastic laugh. "You've always got girls around you like bees around a bunch of flowers. And I know they can't all be shape-shifters. Tell me about it, Alex. How can you be with them and not change like I just did?"

Alex didn't answer right away. He strolled over to where Holly was standing and Holly couldn't help but notice that he looked fabulous. She couldn't deny that.

Alex always looked fabulous.

He was wearing the dark green sweater Holly had knitted for him to wear on New Year's Eve. The color suited him to perfection. It brought out the inky high-lights in his hair and all the different shades of green in his eyes. It fit like a glove, thanks to Holly's mom's knitting know-how and endless hours of ripping out stitches it had taken endless hours to knit.

He looked fabulous, all right.

Until he got closer.

The closer Alex got, the stranger he looked.

Holly passed her hands over her eyes. It was a trick of the light, she told herself. An optical illusion caused by her exhaustion and her worry and the pain and surprise of her change.

But when she moved her hands, Alex still looked weird.

It was as if, for one terrifying minute, Holly saw two Alexes.

One was the Alex she loved. Handsome. Charming. Sophisticated.

The other . . .

Holly shivered and tried to close her eyes. But she couldn't look away. She couldn't do anything but stand and stare.

The other Alex surfaced from somewhere inside the real Alex, like one of those hologram ghosts Holly had seen in the movies. He looked like a ghost, too, or at least like what Holly supposed a ghost would look like. He was an exact carbon copy of Alex. Same face. Same hair. Same clothes. But this Alex was cold looking and blue and Holly could clearly see the real Alex right through him.

When they were within three feet of Holly, there was some sort of power surge. The cold blue halo that surrounded the other Alex flared and flamed and got so white and bright, Holly had to squint.

The creature got bigger. Bulkier. Pretty soon, Holly couldn't see the real Alex through him. All she could see was the creature. He didn't have Alex's face anymore, either. He didn't have any face at all. He didn't have any form. He was made of raw power like the kind that crackles around a downed electric line.

The charge made the hair on Holly's arms stand on end. It vibrated through her skin. She slumped back and held her hands up in front of her face to ward off the creature. But still, the thing that was Alex—but wasn't—came closer until she could feel her skin sizzle with its heat.

"You want to know how I can be with human girls? I'll tell you." Whatever the thing was, it used Alex's voice to send the words directly into her mind. *"I've had years of practice. You haven't. Do you need it spelled out even more clearly, Holly? Let me put it to you this way. If you're with Jason and he kisses you, you'll change. I guarantee you, you'll change. And when you do, you'll rip out his throat."*

The words filled Holly's head. She was still listening to them when she fell on the floor in a dead faint.

4

"Holly! Holly! Wake up."

Holly heard a voice that sounded like it came from the bottom of a deep hole. She felt a gentle slap against her cheek. "Are you okay? Holly?"

Her eyes fluttered open.

She was on the floor of the gazebo, staring up at what was left of the single lightbulb that hung from the rafters.

Holly closed her eyes and tried to pull together the memories of what happened in those last few minutes before she passed out.

No matter how hard she tried, she couldn't remember much of anything. Her thoughts were as scattered as the funny-shaped pieces of a jigsaw puzzle.

She knew that Alex was with her. And then he wasn't. He was gone, and in his place was a being of such power . . .

A chilling cold filled Holly's body and turned her blood to ice water.

It was awful. Too awful. And she didn't want to think about it.

Opening her eyes, Holly concentrated on the lightbulb instead. A blast of air sent it swinging from side to side. She couldn't remember anything happening to the lightbulb, but something must have gone on while she was unconscious. Something incredible. All that was left of the bulb was a ring of broken glass, as jagged and dangerous looking as a dragon's teeth. The rest of the bulb was gone. Shattered. Like it had exploded from the inside.

Gingerly, Holly turned her head from left to right.

Something had happened to the gazebo, too. All around her, the floor was charred as if there'd been a fire.

"At least you're awake. I was worried about you!"

Holly looked up. Alex was bending over her.

The feeling of horror that filled her insides slowly melted away, and Holly's lips lifted in a weak smile.

He was Alex. Just Alex. And there was no one else here. No other creature that wrapped itself around him and spoke with his voice. Just Alex, and there was an expression so tender on his face, it made her heart skip a beat.

"What happened?" Holly's voice sounded scratchy, like sandpaper.

"I don't know." Alex shook his head. "I really don't know. You were fine, then . . . well, I guess you got a little hysterical. You started mumbling something about a monster or a ghost or a creature of some sort. I came over to see what was wrong, but the closer I got, the more upset you got. You screamed and then you fainted. The whole thing didn't take more than a couple minutes, but it felt like days. Are you really all right, Holly?"

Holly sat up. Instantly, Alex wrapped his arms

around her. She was glad. She needed Alex's support right now. She needed the feel of his arms around her, the sound of his heart beating hard and steady in her ears.

"But what about . . . ?" She looked up at the shattered lightbulb. She looked down at the blackened floor. "This isn't hysterical. It's . . . it's . . ." She couldn't find the words. "I wasn't hysterical," she whispered, but she wasn't sure if she was trying to convince Alex or herself. "It *was* some sort of monster. Some monster, and it tried to destroy you." Holly ran her hands over Alex's face.

"But you're all right, aren't you?" She kissed him, quick and hard, and tried to smile through the tears that suddenly filled her eyes and choked her voice. "You're fine. Whatever it was . . . it didn't get you? It didn't hurt you? Please, Alex, tell me you're okay."

For an instant, Holly could have sworn Alex's face darkened, like he was worried about something. It was hard to tell, especially with the light gone. But the next second he was smiling at her. She was sure of that. And that was all that mattered.

"I'm fine. Scout's honor." He raised up one hand. "I don't know what happened here." He looked around at the gazebo. "All I know is that you screamed and then there was some sort of blast. Like an explosion. But I swear to you, there was nobody here but us. No monster. No ghost. Just us."

"I'm so glad." Holly tucked her head against Alex's shoulder. "I must have been dreaming or something." A sudden thought struck her and she sat up.

"You don't think it will happen again, do you? You don't think"—she swallowed hard—"you don't think Laila had something to do with this?"

"If she did, she'll have to answer to me. And I promise you, I won't go easy on her." Alex stood. He took Holly's hands and pulled her to her feet.

"I'll have a talk with her when I get home," he promised. He held Holly at arm's length and looked her up and down.

"You okay?" he asked. "Everything working? Nothing broken?"

Holly flexed her legs and stretched her neck. "I don't think so." She rubbed the back of her head and winced. "I think I got a goose egg when I hit the floor."

Gently, Alex felt around the sore spot. "It'll be even bigger by tomorrow." He dropped a gentle kiss on the back of her head. "You'd better get some ice on it. Come on. I'll walk you home."

"You call this writing!" Her hands on her hips, Laila Sarandon swung around from center stage and stared into the first row of auditorium seats, right at Jason. She held up her script for *Dracula Meets the Los Gatos Panther*. Her top lip curled. "I can't say these lines. They're dumb. And worse than that, they're boring. Every last person in the audience will be asleep before Act Two ever starts."

The anger in Laila's voice was enough to pull Holly's attention away from her homework. She wasn't on stage at all in this scene and she had decided to use the time between play practice and when she was supposed to meet Tisha to catch up on her American history. Now, she snapped her history book shut and sat back to watch the first round of what she was afraid was going to turn into a rip-roaring fight.

Jason untangled himself from the heap of scripts, scenery sketches, and costumes on his lap. He rose from his seat, unfolded his long legs, and stretched. He obviously didn't realize there was a costume caught in his belt buckle. It was one of the dresses meant to be worn at the fancy dress ball in Act Three. It was pink and full of sequins and it glittered around Jason's knees every time he moved. "It's part of the comedy," Jason said. Like it would help Laila understand, he spoke loud and slow. "Don't you get it? The lines are supposed to be funny!"

When he got no reaction from Laila, he looked over at Alex.

"It's supposed to be funny," Jason said. "The lines are funny. Right?"

Alex perched himself on the edge of the battered dining room table that, painted gold, would soon be the banquet table in the ballroom of Dracula's castle. He gave his sister a lazy, disinterested look. "I have no problem with the lines," he said.

Just as Holly suspected it would, Alex's attitude caused Laila to go up like a rocket. She rounded on her brother.

"You have no problem! That's because your little sweetie's over there in the audience." She threw a look to where Holly was sitting in the back of the auditorium. Holly sunk deeper into the red plush seat, sure that her face was the same color as her chair.

"All you want to do is impress her," Laila went on. "All you want to do is show her what a big, bad guy you can be. Dracula!" Laila snorted. "You couldn't suck the blood out of a tomato!"

Dangerously calm, Alex rose from the table and went to stand within a few inches of Laila. He was taller than her by a full half-foot, but other than that, they were nearly carbon copies of each other.

Same ink black hair. Same flashing green eyes.

It was like watching two halves of the same whole square off against each other.

But even though they were so much alike, Laila's power was no match for Alex's. Holly knew that. She saw Laila take a step back when Alex came nearer. It wasn't much, but Alex took advantage of it.

"All I want to do is finish rehearsal so I can go home," he said. His voice was as silky smooth as ice cream. And just as cold. "That would be a lot easier if we didn't have to put up with your infantile tantrums."

"Tantrums?" Laila stomped her foot. "You haven't seen tantrums, pal. I—"

"All right. All right." Jason must have seen what was coming. He waved his hands to get their attention. The pink dress sparkled. "Why don't we just get back to the play, huh? Alex, you've just flown into Camilla's room in the form of a bat. There's a puff of smoke—" Jason looked over at the prop crew. They were lined up backstage watching the fight.

"You guys can do smoke, can't you?" he asked. Satisfied when someone nodded, Jason turned back to Alex. "There's a puff of smoke and you change into Dracula. You glide across the room until you're only inches from Camilla. She looks up at you and says..." He looked at Laila expectantly. "And says..."

"I can't say these lines!" Laila screamed. Jason groaned. Alex shook his head in disgust and went back to sit on the table.

By this time, just about everyone working on the play had gathered to watch the fight. Holly looked up and saw the lighting people hanging over the balcony. The costume crew materialized from backstage, and Holly saw Tisha watching the whole thing. She had a black cape in one hand, a needle and thread in the other.

Laila had an audience and Holly knew what would happen now. She'd play the crowd for all it was worth.

"Listen to this." Laila flipped through the pages of her script until she found what she was looking for. She threw a look at her audience. "Just listen to this." She started to read, her voice as melodramatic as the broad gestures she was making.

" 'Dearest Drac, don't you know how I long to be with you? When you are out in the dark hunting your prey, can't you feel me there at your side, eager to take part in the feast?' " Laila threw back her head and gave a scornful snort of laughter. "It's trash," she screamed, and she flung her script straight at Jason's head. It missed, but only by a couple inches.

Jason let go a low whistle, but he never moved a muscle. Holly had to give him credit. He didn't seem nearly as angry as she was getting.

This play was Jason's baby, his creation. He'd spent hours and hours writing it and he was committed to spending more hours getting it ready for an audience. Laila had a lot of nerve making fun of it, especially in front of the entire cast and crew.

Holly knew that Jason wasn't the only reason she was angry. She was angry for herself, too. She was angry because Laila was supposed to be her friend. She was embarrassed because Laila was causing a scene in front of Jason and Tisha and all the other kids who were Holly's friends before she became a member of Alex's pack.

The tips of Holly's fingers tingled. Her eyes narrowed and suddenly, she picked up Laila's scent. She knew what was happening. Her anger was getting out of control. It was causing the change. She had to defuse it. Fast.

Holly sprang out of her seat and hurried down the aisle to the stage. She got there just in time to see Jason shake his head and look down at the script lying at his feet. "That thing nearly beaned me!" he said.

Laila tossed her head just enough to make her hair gleam in the overhead lights. "Good. Maybe it would have knocked some sense into you. Then you wouldn't even think about giving lines like that to the leading lady in this low-grade farce. Really! How any actress could be caught dead saying stuff like this is beyond me.''

''Maybe it's because you're not much of an actress!''

Holly had no idea her voice could carry so far. But it must have. Every single person in the place was staring right at her. She didn't care. She raised her chin and smiled over at Alex who gave her a heart-stopping smile back.

Laila wasn't smiling. She was staring at Holly with her mouth open. ''What? You've got a part as big as a flea and you're telling me about acting! I suppose you'd like to take over for me. Is that it? You'd like to step in and take over my role here just like you took over—''

''What a great idea!'' Before Laila had a chance to say any more, Alex stepped forward. Like a ringmaster at a circus, he waved his arms and raised his voice, diverting everyone's attention from what Laila was about to say. ''That's it, Jason. Don't you see? Laila hates her part. Let's give it to Holly. She'd be a great Camilla.''

Jason wasn't convinced. ''Oh, I don't know . . .'' He looked at Holly, waiting for her to protest.

She didn't. Only because she didn't know what to say.

''There's an awful lot of lines to learn.'' Jason was trying to scare her off and Holly knew why. Dracula and Camilla had plenty of scenes together and she was sure Jason didn't want to give her that much opportunity to be with Alex.

''Holly can learn them. She can learn anything.'' The more reluctant Jason sounded, the more excited

Alex got about his plan. "I already know most of my lines," he told Jason, and Holly knew it was true. Alex had a remarkable memory. "I'll help Holly learn hers. It'll give us something to do when we're alone together."

That comment was met with snickers from just about everyone watching. Holly felt her face get hot.

"I don't know . . ." Jason's face was red, too. He looked over at Laila and Holly realized he was hoping to find an ally there.

He didn't.

Laila sneered at Holly. "She couldn't act if her life depended on it. But what difference does it make? With lines like these, no one will be here long enough to find out. They'll be running for the exit doors within the first couple minutes anyway."

Jason's face fell. He turned to Holly and played his last card. "And what about cheerleading practice? If you're here every day, how are you going to make it to cheerleading practice?"

"The basketball season will be over a week or two before the play is scheduled," Alex piped in. "This won't interfere at all with cheerleading. Besides" —he raised his eyebrows— "you wrote some really great stuff in the original script. Remember? Stuff you had to take out when you decided to cast me and Laila opposite each other." Alex picked up a script that was sitting in the middle of the banquet table. There were some extra pages stuffed into the middle of it and he flipped through them until he found what he was looking for.

He came back to the center of the stage and started

to read, his voice clear and low and so hypnotic, it held them all under its spell.

" 'Dracula picks up a goblet from a nearby table, drinks from it, then hands it to Camilla. She drinks deeply and tosses the cup aside. Dracula lowers his mouth to her lips and then to her neck. When he raises his head again, his lips are ringed with blood.' "

Alex looked up from his script and smiled one of those slow, lazy smiles that always made Holly's heart feel like it was in meltdown.

"It's great stuff," he said. He came over to the front of the stage and crouched down so that he was looking at Jason eye to eye. He wasn't reading anymore, but his voice still sounded the way it did when he was. Quiet. Soothing. Hypnotic.

"Really great stuff. Stuff you can't leave in if Laila stays on as Camilla. But Holly . . ." Alex sighed and just the sound of it made Holly feel tingly all over.

She looked around and realized she wasn't the only one caught by the magic of Alex's voice. Jason didn't move a muscle and the cast and crew were so quiet, they might have all turned into statues. Even Laila didn't budge.

"Holly's another story," Alex went on. "Give her Camilla's part and the whole thing will be better. More dramatic. More realistic."

"More dramatic. More realistic." Jason repeated the words. His voice sounded funny, kind of hollow, like a zombie in a movie.

"A better play," Alex said.

"A much better play," Jason responded.

Looking very satisfied, Alex hopped to his feet. He brushed his hands together and raised his voice. "Okay, it's settled! Holly's our new Camilla!"

It was like someone flipped a switch and brought all the statues back to life again. There was a sprinkling of applause from the prop crew. The guys handling the lighting got back to work. The costume crew disappeared backstage.

Laila looked like she was about to blow her cork. Her eyes square on Alex, her jaw tight, she said, "Isn't anyone going to ask me?"

"Seems to me you've already resigned." Alex stepped between Laila and the front of the stage. He pointed to the floor at Jason's feet. "That's your script down there, isn't it?"

Laila didn't say a thing. With another toss of her head, and a look that would have withered anyone but Alex, she stomped off the stage.

Jason bent down to retrieve Laila's script. The pink dress wiggled around him like a glistening Jell-O mold. "Congratulations," he said to Holly. He juggled the script from hand to hand. "Looks like you're our new star."

Jason's voice wasn't much more cheerful than his expression. He looked like he'd just been driven over by a piece of heavy machinery.

Holly knew why. By giving her Camilla's part, Jason had guaranteed that Holly and Alex would spend hours and hours together between now and the play. He'd agreed to throw them together on and off the stage. He'd authorized them to practice that passionate kiss and he knew he'd have to watch them do it every time.

Jason was confused. Holly could tell from the look in his eyes. He'd just been talked into something he had no intention of ever doing and it was pretty clear he didn't understand how Alex did it.

Neither did Holly.

She shot a look in Alex's direction, but he wasn't paying attention. He'd already gathered his books and his coat and was heading for the door.

"Yeah. Looks like I am." Holly snatched the script from Jason's hands and turned to hurry after Alex.

He was already out in the hallway when she caught up to him. She grabbed onto his coat sleeve and held him in place.

"What's the deal?" She shot the question at him.

"Deal?" Alex looked at her like she was talking Chinese. "What are you talking about?"

"I'm talking about that." Holly stabbed one finger in the direction of the auditorium. "I didn't want that part. You know that. And Jason didn't want to give it to me. But he did. You made him. I don't know how. But you did. You made everybody in there believe that it was the best thing to do."

Alex shrugged and smiled. "So? Now we have a perfect excuse for spending more time together. You have a lot of lines to memorize. I'll come by after dinner and—"

"I'm going to Gino's with Tisha tonight."

Alex's smile disappeared. "It's probably not a

good idea,'' he said. ''You know how being with humans can confuse you.''

Holly heard what he was saying but she couldn't believe it. ''Humans?'' She fought to keep her voice down. ''Humans don't confuse me nearly as much as you do. One minute you tell me it's okay to spend time with Tisha, the next minute you say it will confuse me. One minute you tell me to stay away from Jason, the next minute, you practically shove us together. Does any of this make sense to you, Alex? 'Cause it sure doesn't to me.''

If there was one thing Holly knew about Alex, it was that he never let his emotions get the best of him. To anyone else, she was sure he looked perfectly cool as he listened to her rant and rave. His expression was composed. His eyes were calm. His posture was loose and relaxed.

But Holly knew that Alex was angry. Very angry.

She could tell from the fierce way he rubbed the tips of his fingers against his rough wool jacket, like they itched and nothing he did could make it stop. She could tell because she was mad, too, and the emotion sharpened her senses.

She caught the scent of Alex's anger. It stuck in the back of her throat. It rushed through her bloodstream. It made her canine teeth tingle.

The urge to change was strong in Holly, but this time she held it back. She wasn't sure how. She wasn't sure where she got the strength or the skill. She only knew she was directing the change. For the first time, she had total control.

She willed her face to change.

And it did.

Holly saw a powerful panther reflected in Alex's eyes.

She willed her hands to transform.

And they did.

Holly swiped her razor-sharp claws at Alex. She wasn't near enough to injure him in any way. It was just a warning.

And it worked.

Holly caught the strong, spicy scent of surprise coming from him.

It didn't take Alex long to figure out that Holly had won. At least this time. That was enough to erase his surprise and make his anger come thundering back, full strength.

Holly staggered back against the force of his fury. Alex could have destroyed her then. She was sure of it. With one movement of his hand, he could have wiped her out.

Instead, he swung around and headed for the door. When he got there, he turned and smiled at Holly. It wasn't his usual smile, not the kind that made her feel warm inside. This was a predator's smile. It was smooth and sleek and it flashed over Alex's mouth and reflected in his eyes like lightning. "Just be careful around Tisha," Alex said. "If anyone can get you talking, it would be her. And Jason? You don't have a thing to worry about there. All you have to do is make sure you never kiss him!"

5

"So you're the new star of the play?"

It was the fourth time that Tisha asked the same thing.

"Yeah."

It was the fourth time Holly gave her the same answer.

They hadn't been together for more than five minutes and already they'd run out of things to talk about.

Both their heads down, both their hands stuffed in their pockets, Holly and Tisha walked side by side across the Los Gatos town square, headed in the direction of Gino's.

Holly watched her breath float out in front of her like a frosty cloud.

It was going to be a long afternoon.

It wasn't like last fall, when she and Tisha were best friends. They never got tired of talking then. They never had to fill the quiet spots between their conversations with awkward words.

All this polite beating around the bush wasn't doing much for Holly's mood. She couldn't forget the look on Alex's face when he made that parting shot at school. And she couldn't forget how mad he'd made her.

It was their first fight. And it still hurt. A lot.

Holly frowned. "I don't feel much like a star," she admitted.

"You don't?" Tisha pulled to a stop and looked at her in wonder. "I mean, I figured you would. You've been going with Alex for how long now? Any girl who goes out with him must automatically think of herself as the center of the universe. That's how he acts. That's how he treats you."

"Alex treats me great," Holly answered a little too quickly. She wondered if she was trying to convince Tisha or herself. She slapped the doubts out of her mind and changed the subject before Tisha could notice how uncomfortable it made her. "I just don't think I'll like getting up there in front of all those people. Or memorizing all those lines. And Jason—"

Tisha's lips thinned. She grumbled something under her breath and, without waiting until they got as far as the corner crosswalk, she charged across the street. "Don't tell me you care what Jason's feeling," she said over her shoulder. "I can't believe that."

Holly was so stunned by the comment, she couldn't even move. She stood frozen by surprise and watched Tisha walk farther and farther away. A car came by and splashed water on Holly's shoes. She jumped. "Believe it," she yelled. She darted a look both ways and hurried to catch up to Tisha. She was yelling her reply before she was halfway there. "I like Jason.

You know that. I've always liked Jason. I don't want to see him suffer.''

''You think you can practice those steamy Dracula and Camilla scenes in front of him and not see him suffer?'' Tisha was still walking. Fast. Each of her words was punctuated by her footsteps. ''Don't tell me, let me guess, you're going to say you just can't walk away from your one true love, is that it?''

''Yes. That is it.'' Holly's voice was just as sharp as Tisha's. She fell into step beside her and kept up with no problem at all. ''I am in love with Alex. And he's in love with me. I know you don't like Alex so I know you don't understand. But he's not a bad person. Not at all. There's so much to like about him once you get to know him better. There's a lot . . . there's a lot you don't know about him, Tisha.'' With one hand, Holly grabbed onto Tisha's shoulder. She stopped her.

''There's a lot you don't know about me,'' Holly told her. ''But we're alike, me and Alex, and we're meant to be together. Whether you like it or not. Whether Jason likes it or not. Nothing's going to change that. And I don't see why it should. I'm sorry we're not friends anymore. I'm sorry Jason isn't happy. But that doesn't mean I'm going to give up Alex, just to make the two of you feel better. That wouldn't be fair and you know it.''

For a minute Tisha didn't say anything. Holly knew she wanted to. Her eyes were scrunched up. Her hands were bunched into fists. Tisha had an opinion about everything and most times she couldn't wait to express it.

Holly stood back and waited.

But the lecture never came.

After a couple of seconds, Tisha's eyes flew wide open. She was so excited, she grabbed onto Holly's sleeve and hopped up and down. "Holly! Do you realize what's happening? We're arguing! We're talking! We're not just trading polite phrases. We're really talking. Like in the old days!"

Tisha was right.

Holly felt her unhappiness melt in the sunshine of Tisha's friendly smile. All she could do was smile back.

Wrapping her arm through Tisha's, Holly led the way to Gino's.

"Do you suppose two people who argue can ever be friends like they used to be?" Tisha asked. Her voice was as bouncy as her walk suddenly was.

"I think they can try," Holly said. And she meant it.

They were almost all the way across the square when the gazebo caught Tisha's eye. "Did you hear about the fire the other night?" she asked. "I've tried to get the lowdown from the guys up at the fire station and the people at police headquarters, but they don't seem to know much. Or if they do, they're not talking."

Holly didn't reply. She didn't want to see the gazebo. She didn't want to think about it. Just looking at the place made her stomach feel queasy. No matter how hard she tried, she just couldn't forget the frightening hallucination she'd seen there.

But Tisha was determined to explore, especially when she saw a man in a dark coat come around from the back side of the gazebo. "Look!" She pulled Holly toward the structure. "There's Chief Radley from the fire department. Looks like he's checking things out. Let's see what we can find out."

Holly thought the memory of the incident a couple nights ago was etched in her brain forever. But the closer they got, the more she realized her memory wasn't very clear. The damage was a lot worse than she remembered. The wooden floor of the gazebo was charred. She remembered that. But the columns that held up the roof were black, and she didn't recall that at all. Some of the rafters were scorched, too.

It made an odd picture. The outside of the gazebo was as pretty as ever. Its white paint looked pearly in the late afternoon light. But the inside was burned to a crisp. The whole thing reminded Holly of a roasted marshmallow turned inside out.

Tisha dragged Holly all the way up to the yellow fire department tape that was wrapped around the gazebo. She was talking to Chief Radley before she got there. "Figure out what happened yet?"

The chief pushed his cloth cap farther back on his head. "Strangest thing I've ever seen." He scratched his head. "Not much real damage. Just a lot of burn marks. Won't take more than a good scraping and a coat of paint to fix it up again. What I can't figure is why anyone would do it. Or how they did it without demolishing the place. Fire usually eats its way right through wood as old as this.''

Holly poked at the bottom step of the gazebo with the tip of her shoe. It was crazy of her to even bring it up, but suddenly she needed to find out all she could about the fire. Almost afraid to hear what the chief had to say, she asked, ''You don't have any leads on who did it, do you?''

''Not a one.'' Chief Radley shook his head. ''Must have happened late. No one was around. All we know is what started it.''

''You do?'' Holly couldn't have been more surprised. She was there, and she didn't know for sure what started it, except that it was something cold and blue and it looked like Alex until it evaporated into some kind of fiery explosion.

Somehow, she didn't think that was the same explanation the chief was going to give.

She was right. Chief Radley pointed to something sitting in the center of the floor. ''Near as we can figure, that's what started all the trouble.''

There in the middle of the gazebo sat all that was left of a small stack of papers. It wasn't completely burned. Some of the sheets were still whole. They were black and crisp.

''Can't figure out what it is,'' the chief said. ''Not that it matters. Somebody started the paper on fire and that must be what burned the rest of the place.'' He looked up at the rafters. ''The heat couldn't have been strong enough to burst that lightbulb, though. Maybe it's been broken for a while and no one noticed.''

Holly looked at the burned papers and a lump formed in her throat. Maybe the fire department didn't know exactly what the blackened pile of papers was, but she sure did.

It was the script for *Dracula Meets the Los Gatos Panther.* It had been incinerated by the power of the creature's hatred.

By the time they finished their pizza and got back to her house, Tisha was laughing and talking just like the old days.

If she noticed Holly was kind of quiet, she didn't show it. She kept chattering on and on, and Holly was glad. At least Tisha's gossip helped take her mind off the horrible memory that kept popping into her head: a picture of the burned script, its pages fluttering in the icy breeze.

Still telling Holly a story about classmate Mark Latimer and his big fight with Donna Pool, his latest girlfriend, Tisha showed Holly where to leave her shoes near the front door and led the way upstairs. It wasn't common knowledge that Mark was dumping his girlfriend, Tisha was quick to point out. In fact, Donna didn't even know yet.

Holly could only shake her head in amazement.

Tisha wasn't known as the Tisha News Network for nothing. She really was the TNN. And she really did know everything. About everybody.

Finishing up the story, Tisha pushed open her bedroom door and snapped on the light. "I figured we'd stop by here after Gino's so I cleaned," she said. She swept her arm over the room. "Not bad, huh? I got most of my clothes shoved into my dresser drawers. Just about everything else is under the bed."

Holly followed her into the room. She stopped just inside the doorway and wrinkled her nose. She waved one hand in front of her face. "What is that smell?"

Tisha sniffed the air. "I don't smell anything." She caught herself. "Oh wait! It must be the pennyroyal. I'm so used to it, I don't even smell it anymore."

"Pennyroyal?" Cautiously, Holly took a breath. It wasn't a bad smell. Just kind of odd. It smelled minty, like the herbal tea Holly's mom sometimes drank before she went to bed.

Shrugging out of her coat, Tisha went over to her dresser and fished through the bottles of perfume, makeup, and bath gel that covered it. She smiled when she found what she was looking for. "I got it at a health food store over in Portland," she said. She held up a small glass bottle with some kind of dark, oily-looking stuff inside. "I use it on myself every morning and I rub it all around the room every night before I go to bed."

"You do?" Holly slipped off her jacket and hung it over the nearest chair. She gave Tisha a questioning look. "Why?"

Tisha gripped the little bottle directly in front of her. Her face was very solemn. "You can't be too careful," she said.

Holly was more confused than ever. Trying to figure out what was going on, she went over to the wide window that took up most of one wall of Tisha's room. It was long past dark and, with the room lights on, Holly could barely see the big old oak tree she knew stood right outside the window. She could see Tisha, though, reflected in the glass. She looked as serious as ever. She was holding onto the bottle of pennyroyal for dear life.

Something hanging above the window caught Holly's eye. She stood on tiptoe and took a closer look. "Tisha!" Holly couldn't believe her eyes. "There's garlic hanging from your curtain rod."

Tisha didn't seem to think that was the least bit peculiar. "Of course," she said. "I told you, you can't be too careful."

Holly wasn't sure what Tisha expected her to say. For a couple seconds, she groped around for the right words. That didn't work. There wasn't a right way to ask someone why they rubbed strange-smelling oil all over their room and hung bulbs of garlic from their curtains rods, Holly decided. All she could do was come right out and say it. She went over to where Tisha was standing and looked her in the eye. "What is this all about?"

Tisha glanced at the window. She looked over her shoulder at her closed bedroom door. She leaned closer to Holly and lowered her voice. "Panthers," she said.

"Panthers." The single word made Holly's heart thump against her ribs. Because she didn't want Tisha to guess how much the subject meant to her, Holly turned away. She pretended to be really interested in one of the posters that hung on Tisha's wall. It was a picture of Vanilla Fish, Tisha's favorite rock group, and Holly took a lot of time studying each of the singers' faces.

Her eyes still on the poster, she asked, "What panthers are those?"

Throwing her hands in the air, Tisha started flapping around the room. "What do you mean, what panthers?" She zipped past Holly on her way to the window. When she got there, she flipped around and came back the other way. There were spots of bright color in her cheeks that matched her red sweatshirt exactly. "How can you even ask that? How can you ask what panthers? It's not exactly a mysterious top secret, is it? You know what panthers I'm talking about!"

Holly didn't like the sound of this at all. There was no way Tisha could know about Alex and the other shape-shifters, she told herself. Even if she was the TNN, there was no way Tisha could know this secret.

Or could she?

In the last few months, Holly had learned so much about the special Gift she shared with the six other shape-shifters. She could recognize the signs of her own anger now. She could identify the smell of fear. She could distinguish the tangy bite of excitement. And the bitter aroma of jealousy. And the sweet fragrance of Alex's affection.

But here in Tisha's room, she caught a new scent. One she recognized instantly. One she didn't like at all.

It made her nose itch. It caused a slow shiver to

crawl up her spine and triggered warning bells in her head.

It was the smell of danger.

Holly took a long look at Tisha. Was it her imagination, or was there more in Tisha's brown, almond-shaped eyes than innocence? Did Tisha know something? Something she had no business knowing?

Holly's teeth tingled. It was a natural reaction, she told herself, trying to ease the sudden panic that filled her when she realized what was happening. It was a natural response to feeling threatened, an instinctive reaction to Tisha's vague hints about panthers and secrets. Still, it had to stop. Holly knew that. It had to stop. No matter what.

If Tisha didn't know about the shape-shifters, Holly couldn't risk changing and letting her find out.

And if she did know?

Holly didn't want to think about what she might have to do then.

Shaking away the disturbing questions, trying her best to act casual, Holly went over to Tisha's bed and sat down on the black-and-white bedspread. Wide-eyed, she looked at Tisha. "*I* know what panthers you're talking about? Me?"

"Of course you do!" Tisha was exasperated. She plopped down on the bed next to Holly. Without batting an eyelash, she said simply, "The ones that got Mr. Tollifson."

"Oh!" Holly let go of a long, ragged breath. She scraped the tips of her fingers back and forth over the bedspread. "Are you sure you're not just mixing up what happened to Mr. Tollifson with all that nonsense about the Los Gatos panther legend?'' she asked. ''It's just a story, you know.''

''Just a story!'' Tisha sat up straight as an arrow. ''How can you say that? You know what happened to Mr. Tollifson. They found him ripped to pieces. There was blood all over Harper's Mountain. Blood in the grass. Blood on that goofy animal trap of his. I hear there was even a trail of blood leading from the center of Panther Hollow all the way to where they found his body. He was stuffed up in a tree. Remember, Holly? That's how panthers hunt.''

It was how panthers hunted.

A couple minutes ago, the possibility that Tisha had guessed her secret was the most important thing in the world to Holly. Suddenly it didn't seem that critical anymore. Maybe Tisha had guessed her secret. What she couldn't possibly have guessed was what all this talk about Mr. Tollifson's blood was doing to Holly.

Her ears were buzzing. Her face was hot. Her stomach growled and her mouth and lips puckered like they did when she ate something sour. Holly ran her tongue over her lips. They'd just finished eating a large pizza, she reminded herself. They'd just finished drinking two big pitchers of Coke. They'd just finished sharing an extra-large hot fudge sundae with peanuts and whipped cream and strawberry wafers on the side.

And she was hungry.

Very hungry.

The realization hit Holly with all the force of a fast-moving freight train. She batted it aside and forced her attention back to Tisha just in time to see Tisha cross her arms over her chest.

"Maybe it's just a story to you," Tisha was saying, "but I'm not taking any chances. And you shouldn't, either."

Tisha hopped off the bed. She unscrewed the top of the pennyroyal bottle, tipped it against her hand, and reached her gleaming, oily fingers toward Holly. "Here," she said. "Let me put some of this on you. Just a dab behind the ears. Like perfume."

Holly ducked. "Yuk! It smells like wet weeds." Rolling over on her side toward the far end of the bed, she dodged Tisha's outstretched hand. "I don't want to smell like that!"

"You don't want to get gobbled up by panthers, do you?" Tisha sounded just like Holly's mother did when she was trying to get her to eat something awful, like lima beans. "Just a little bit?" Tisha pushed her hand toward Holly again. She looked so sincere. So innocent.

The thought gave Holly a glimmer of hope. Tisha couldn't know about the shape-shifters, Holly told herself. If she did, she wouldn't be offering Holly protection from them.

"Oh, all right." Holly tried her best not to sound too relieved. She swept her hair away from her neck and let Tisha dab some of the oil behind her ears. This close, the pennyroyal smelled weirder than ever. But that was okay. At least the strange smell had taken Holly's mind off her stomach.

She smoothed her hair back down and hoped she had the chance to wash the pennyroyal off before her parents smelled it and asked what it was. "What makes you think this stuff will work?" she asked.

Tisha shrugged. She wiped her hands against her sweatshirt and recapped the bottle. "I don't," she said. "But I figured it was better than doing nothing. I read somewhere that herbal flea collars are great for dogs, but you can't use them around cats if they have pennyroyal in them." When it looked like Holly didn't follow, Tisha rolled her eyes. "Don't you get it? Pennyroyal makes cats sick. And if it makes cats sick, I figure it does the same thing for panthers."

Holly hated to tell her how wrong she was. All the pennyroyal was doing to this panther was making her think of herb tea. Almost afraid to hear the answer, Holly asked, "And the garlic?"

"Well, it keeps vampires away, doesn't it?"

There wasn't much Holly could say about that. She shouldn't be surprised by all this, Holly thought. Tisha always was the one person in Los Gatos who really believed the panther legend. It was only natural after the way Mr. Tollifson died that she should be more afraid than ever. It was too bad she had to feel that way.

Holly slid off the bed and went to the window. She fingered the garlic. "What does your grandmother say about all this?"

"She doesn't know. I don't want her to worry."

Holly watched Tisha's reflection in the glass. "Look," she said, "I don't think you have to worry, either. I mean, I don't think there's anything for you to be afraid of.''

Holly couldn't tell an out-and-out lie. But she couldn't tell the whole truth, either. Instead, she decided she'd be happy if she could just calm Tisha's fears. She wanted to let her know she was certain no panther would ever threaten Tisha or her grandmother.

''Even if there is a Los Gatos panther,'' Holly started to say . . .

She never had the chance to finish.

The words stuck in Holly's throat and she stared out the window. For a moment, she wondered if she wasn't dreaming again. Was that her face she saw staring back at her?

No.

Holly clearly saw her own face mirrored in the window, her eyes round with surprise. Over her left shoulder she saw Tisha at her dresser putting the bottle of pennyroyal back where it belonged.

Thank goodness.

Tisha was so busy straightening all the bottles and jars, she didn't see what was sitting in the tree right outside her window.

It was a panther.

6

Holly's eyes met Alex's and locked.

"Are you crazy?" The words tumbled out of her before she could stop them.

"What's that?" Tisha looked up from what she was doing.

Holly spun to face her. "I said . . . I said . . . I said I have to go now," she blurted out. She grabbed her coat, wadded it up in her arms and headed for the door.

"You have to go?" Tisha's face got pale. "Hey, I didn't mean to scare you away. If you're uncomfortable . . . I mean, if all this stuff about the garlic and the pennyroyal and all . . . if you think I'm wacko or something . . . I'm sorry, Holly, I—"

"No. I don't think you're crazy." Already halfway out the door, Holly stopped dead. She didn't want Tisha to think she was running away from her. But how could she explain?

She whirled around and gave Tisha a quick hug. "Honest!" she said. "I don't think you're nuts. I just have to go. That's all. Bye!"

Less than a minute later, Holly had her shoes on and was back outside. She paused on the sidewalk in front of Tisha's house to catch her breath and took the time to look up at the big oak tree.

The faint glimmer coming from the window of Tisha's room lit the tree with a pale yellow light that made the bare branches look like skeleton arms.

It wasn't much light, but it was enough. Enough for Holly to see that there was no sign of Alex in the tree.

She looked around.

He wasn't anywhere in the yard, either.

She sniffed the air.

No sign of him.

No sign of any panther.

Holly slipped on her coat and started walking toward home, but not before she looked up at the tree one last time.

Maybe she had imagined Alex sitting there, peering in the window, watching her every move.

The possibility played its way through Holly's head. But by the time she got to the end of the street and turned the corner, it didn't seem to matter much anymore.

Because that's when she saw him.

There was something about seeing Alex when she didn't expect to that always made Holly's head spin and her stomach do flips. It was like tripping over some gorgeous work of art when you were out for your morning walk, or finding something special and unexpected at the bottom of your locker at school.

He always took her breath away.

Tonight was no exception.

Alex had changed into his human shape. He was

leaning against a streetlight. His head was back against the pole, his eyes half-closed. He wasn't wearing a jacket, just dark jeans and a light-colored shirt that glowed like quicksilver in the gleam of the lamp.

This time, the shock of seeing him so suddenly didn't last long. Holly was too angry for that. Shaking away the hypnotic effect he always had on her, she rushed over to where Alex was standing.

"Are you crazy?" she asked him, trying to keep her voice down and not having much luck. She pointed back toward Tisha's house. "She could have seen you."

For a second, Alex didn't respond and Holly wondered if he wasn't asleep. Then she saw the slow smile that crawled around his lips.

"But she didn't see me, did she?" His eyes flickered open. He looked, and sounded, very pleased with himself. "No one sees me unless I want to be seen."

"But I saw you, didn't I?" Holly barely controlled a screech of frustration. She was not in the mood for games. She stuffed her hands in her pockets and headed for home.

It was a couple minutes before she heard Alex's footsteps behind her.

"I didn't mean to scare you." He didn't sound pleased with himself now. He sounded sorry.

"I wasn't scared." Holly didn't look back. She didn't care how he sounded. She wasn't ready to forgive him yet.

"I didn't mean to interrupt your visit with Tisha."

"But you did."

"I wasn't listening."

"I'll bet."

"I don't want you to think that I'm following you or anything. I don't want you to think I'm butting in—"

"But you are, aren't you?" Holly couldn't stand it anymore. She stopped and whirled around so fast that she caught Alex off guard. He slammed right into her.

Holly didn't care. She straightened up and pushed Alex an arm's length away. "You are butting in," she said. "You keep butting in. You couldn't leave me and Tisha alone. You somehow got me the starring part in that play. You're obsessed with the nutty idea that I'm going to grab Jason in some passionate embrace and kiss the living daylights out of him, even though you know I won't. And you are following me. You're following me now. Why can't you just leave me alone?"

"Because I love you."

This time, it was Alex who caught her by surprise. He didn't say another thing. He just smiled the sort of charming, one-sided smile that made the corners of his eyes crinkle.

"What?" Holly finally asked, blinking back to reality.

"I said I love you." Alex took a step nearer. Holly had put on her coat but she hadn't bothered to zip it. He slipped his hands inside and linked his fingers at the small of her back.

"I'm following you now because I love you," he said. "I followed you to Tisha's because I love you. I know I've been a little irrational when it comes to

Jason, but I can't help it. Everything I say, and everything I think and feel and do these days is because I love you."

"Really?" Holly didn't even try to hold on to her anger. How could she when Alex was smiling down at her? "You never said it before."

He made a face that was sheepish and comical and very contrite. "I guess I didn't figure I had to say it. Until this afternoon . . . This afternoon, well, when we had that fight, it brought me to my senses. It made me realize you're the most important thing in the world to me. I waited a lifetime to see you again, Holly. I couldn't stand to live without you."

This time, he didn't wait for her to say anything. He drew her closer and kissed her. Alex's mouth was as warm as the feel of his hands against her back. His kiss was gentle. His touch was so tender, it made Holly's heart ache. She knew she didn't need to say anything. Not tonight. Not ever. Her answer was in her kiss.

"Can I walk you home?" Alex put one arm around her. "Whew!" He wrinkled his nose. "What's that smell?"

"It's pennyroyal. Tisha says . . ." Holly laughed. "Never mind!" She leaned her head on Alex's shoulder. The misery and anger she'd felt only minutes ago was gone. All she felt now was the warmth: the comfort of Alex's smile, the heat of his embrace, the special, wonderful way she felt when she thought about his love.

They didn't say another word for a long time. And Holly was glad.

Though she and Alex had been out together lots of times in the last few months, most of their dates were as much for learning as they were for fun. As soon as they'd left the party or dance or sporting event that was their "date," he'd change into his panther shape and insist that Holly change into hers. Together, they would roam Los Gatos, with Alex taking the time to teach her everything she needed to know about the Gift: how to walk so quietly no one would ever hear her, how to slip in and out of the shadows so no one would ever see her, how to change—quickly, painlessly, instantly—so no one would ever suspect.

But tonight was different.

Tonight, Alex didn't ask her to change.

Holly was glad.

She could be Holly. Just Holly. And she could enjoy the feel of Alex's arm around her, and the quiet, ordinary sound of his footsteps against the sidewalk, and the very human warmth of his hand where it rested on her shoulder.

"This is where your dad teaches, isn't it?" Alex's voice broke through Holly's warm, fuzzy thoughts. She lifted her head and saw they were almost home. The buildings of Los Gatos State University where her dad taught Art History were right across the street. Their house was on the other side of campus.

Holly nodded and let her gaze sweep over the familiar buildings. Los Gatos State was founded more than one hundred years earlier. There were some newer buildings toward the west end of the campus, dorms and laboratories, mostly. That's the part of the college Holly could see from home.

But the buildings up front here near the main administration building and the library were vintage Gothic. They reminded Holly of castles, though she hoped real castles weren't nearly this ugly.

The old buildings were made of enormous blocks of dark stone. Some of them had turrets. Most were covered with ivy. Every single one had a shallow stone stairway that led up to massive wooden doors. The stairs were edged with some kind of bushes— Holly wasn't sure what they were called—that had big, rubbery-looking leaves. She supposed someone a hundred years ago must have thought the plants were attractive. Maybe they were back then. Now, they just looked wild and overgrown.

"Dad's classes aren't up front here," she explained. "He teaches back there." She pointed. "That's where the art museum is. Dad does his research there and teaches a class or two every quarter." She turned to Alex. "You must have been to the museum before. Haven't you been dragged there on field trips?"

"You're the one taking all the art classes. You've been dragged there on field trips." Alex tucked his hands into the pockets of his jeans. He chuckled. "Culture is for you guys planning on going to college and majoring in the arts," he said. "They don't like to waste it on those of us who are only planning on getting our business degrees."

Holly laughed, too.

It was nice, standing here with Alex, sharing a laugh. It made her insides feel warm.

"Let's go take a look at the museum."

Alex's words closed over the warm feeling inside Holly like frost on a flower. But before she could protest, Alex was already on his way across the street.

He looked back to see if Holly was following. "You've never shown me where your dad works. Let's go."

Holly didn't move. She called after him. "If you want to see the museum, we can come any time. I mean, during the day. Dad will be happy to take us around. It will be all closed up now."

But Alex wasn't listening.

His steps as silent as the stars that winked in the sky above Holly's head, he melted into the black shadows between the buildings.

Holly mumbled a word her mother wouldn't approve of. There was no use waiting for Alex to come back. She knew that. Alex was going to check out the museum. His mind was made up. And nothing she could say or do would change it.

With another mumbled curse, Holly crossed the street.

Her night senses were not nearly as keen as Alex's. But they were good enough to point the way through the maze of campus buildings, especially since she'd been here so many times before.

It took her only a couple minutes to get to the museum.

Alex was already there. He was standing still as a statue, staring at the front of the building. Holly took a long look at it, too.

The Henry Cory Clare Museum of Art looked just like all the other old buildings on campus.

Except that it was bigger.

And uglier.

Instead of one tower, it had two, one on each side of the building.

Instead of a shallow stone stairway, it had a set of steep stairs that led up to a door that looked like the drawbridge of a castle.

Instead of having wild-looking plants growing right out front, it had a whole jungle of them. They were lined up on either side of the long walkway that led up to the front steps.

The museum had hundreds of little diamond-paned windows. Even though they were pretty far from the road, the windows picked up the light of every car that went by. When that happened, Holly always thought it looked like someone holding a candle was inside, racing from room to room.

If the rest of the buildings on campus looked like castles, this one went one step further. It looked like a haunted castle, something straight out of a Saturday afternoon B movie. Even in the daytime, Holly didn't like the place. At night, it gave her the creeps.

Holly hugged herself. "Dad says the place is named after a guy named Henry Cory Clare," she said. Did she want Alex to know the story? Or was she just trying to calm the jitters the place always gave her? "A hundred years ago or so, he was the richest guy in Los Gatos. He was also crazy about ancient Egyptian culture and history. After he made his first million or two, he left town and went off to Egypt to dig around the ruins. That's where he died. In his will, he left the university a bundle of money. On one condition. They had to bring over the temple he was excavating. Piece by piece. And they had to reassemble it here. There was a big scandal! The people said a pagan temple in the middle of town was a disgrace. But the university trustees wanted the money. So they reconstructed the temple. Right here, on the spot where Henry Clare wanted it. Then they built the museum around it to cover it up. Dad says no one is sure what Egyptian god the temple honors."

"He's wrong." An expression something like a smile lightened the serious look on Alex's face. "Everyone's wrong. They're too stupid to know."

"I don't see how they could have missed it. I've been inside. The original temple is down in the basement. The walls are covered with carving and writing. Somebody must have studied it all. Scholars can read the hieroglyphs, can't they? The ancient Egyptian picture-writing?"

"Then they didn't look in the right place."

Holly wasn't convinced. "How do you know?" she asked. "You said you've never been here before."

Alex's smile vanished and even though he was looking right at her, Holly was sure he wasn't seeing her. He was looking through her, past her, looking at something that happened long, long ago.

Something extraordinary.

Something mysterious.

Something painful.

"I said I've never been dragged here on field trips," Alex said. His voice sounded as far away as the look in his eyes. "But I've been here before. Believe me. I've been here a thousand times before."

He looked up suddenly, as if someone had called his name. "Come on," he said, grabbing Holly's hand. "Let's go inside."

Alex stopped outside the back door and reached for the doorknob.

"Alex!" Holly yanked his hand away. She kept her voice down to a harsh whisper. "You just can't walk in. I'm sure it's locked. And even if it wasn't, Joe wouldn't let us in. Joe Pendergrast? The night watchman? He has strict instructions from Dad. Nobody's allowed in without authorization after hours. Not even me."

Alex dropped his hand to his side. He looked around. High above them, a window had been left open, probably for ventilation. "Okay," he said. "We'll have to go in that way."

"Alex!" Holly grabbed for him.

It was too late.

In a split-second, he had already changed into his panther shape. As quick as a heartbeat, as quiet as the night, he vaulted toward the open window and disappeared inside the museum.

7

It was easy to move through the museum unnoticed.

There weren't any lights on. Only a spotlight here and there, enough to brighten up an entryway or mark the place where an emergency phone was located.

And if all the lights were on?

A chuckle rumbled through Alex's broad chest.

Even if all the lights were on, no one would see him.

Not if he didn't want to be seen.

Pushing his way through the double doors that separated the classroom part of the building from the museum galleries, Alex continued on toward the doorway that led into the basement temple.

He smiled to himself when he saw it, but he didn't stop when he got there. He didn't look back over his shoulder.

He knew Holly was following him.

He could hear her footsteps.

He could smell her.

From her scent, he knew she was irritated at him for coming into the museum when she asked him not to. He knew that she was afraid, too, afraid someone would find them.

Alex caught another smell.

His nose twitched and a purr vibrated through him.

Holly was excited. He knew that, too.

The thrill of doing something this daring rushed through her. It sent an unmistakable smell into the air, a scent that was intoxicating.

Alex bounded down the steps. He knew Holly would follow him into the basement. She would have to. Because he was excited, too. Excited by the dark. Excited by the risk. Excited by the scents that surrounded him, and the nearness of the temple, and the waves of memory and emotion that always washed over him when he came to this place, memories that touched him all along his body, like hands in the darkness.

His emotions would draw Holly like a lure, just like hers drew him.

She would follow him.

At the bottom of the stairs, Alex paused. Cautiously, he sniffed the air.

There was no sign of Joe the watchman, but Alex knew he'd passed this way not too long ago. He caught the faint, sour smell of Joe's sturdy work shoes and the strong aroma of the onions he'd had on the sandwich he'd eaten for dinner.

Alex congratulated himself on his timing.

If Joe had just been here, he probably wouldn't be back any time soon. And that meant there was no hurry.

Enjoying the moment, Alex sat back. There was a wide hallway at the bottom of the steps and on the other side of it another set of double doors. But unlike the plain wooden doors upstairs, these doors were beautiful.

Magical.

They were made of stone the color of the desert. Even in the dark they seemed to glow, as if the light of the hot Egyptian sun that had shone on them for thousands of years had warmed them through and through.

A rush of pride heated Alex's blood.

Even here, in this dismal basement, the light of the goddess could not be extinguished.

Each of the doors was wider and taller than Alex in his human form. They were cut from solid blocks of stone. During museum operating hours, they were pushed back and left open. But now the doors were closed and Alex took a long look at them. Each door was decorated with a carving of a human, one bringing a plate of fish in his hands, the other carrying a bowl of blood: offerings for the goddess.

"Soon I will bring an offering, too."

Alex said the prayer in his head.

"Soon I will leave a gift to ease your hunger."

He padded across the corridor.

He didn't touch the doors. He didn't have to.

They swung apart.

Silently. Slowly.

Until they were fully open.

He took a deep breath.

With lightning speed Alex changed into his human form and, bowing his head, he walked into the Temple of Bast.

• • •

"This is breaking and entering, you know."

Alex didn't turn around.

Even though it was pitch-black, Holly could see that his back was to her. His hands were clasped in front of him. His head was bent. He just stood there.

Holly took a couple more steps into the temple. She'd been here enough times with her dad to know that there was a stone slab something like an altar over on the far wall. She could just make out Alex standing in front of it. He was as still as one of the statues she knew lined the walls.

She changed into her human form, too.

"I said, it's breaking and entering." Keeping her voice down, Holly moved forward.

His head came up. "I don't remember breaking anything." His voice was as sharp as splintered glass.

Exasperated, Holly grabbed Alex's arm. "No. But we're someplace we shouldn't be. And if we're caught, how are we going to explain how we got in?"

Alex yanked his arm away. "We won't get caught."

It was as simple as that. At least for Alex.

Holly wasn't convinced.

She propped her fists on her hips and glared at him.

Alex glared back.

"Don't you feel it?" he asked. He sounded frustrated, like he was trying to explain something to somebody too hopelessly dumb to understand. "Don't you hear the stones calling your name? Don't you feel the holiness of the place? It's part of you, Holly. And all you can think about is getting caught." He snorted and leaned forward, resting his hands flat against the stone slab. "You're as bad as Laila."

Laila!

Holly stood stock-still. The insult seeped into every fragment of her body.

Alex had compared her to Laila. He couldn't have hurt her more if he slapped her.

Fighting back tears of embarrassment, Holly let herself do something she hadn't done since she transformed into a panther and leapt into the back window to follow Alex into the museum.

She let herself relax.

She told herself to listen.

She allowed herself to feel.

And she knew Alex was right.

Holly moved a step closer to Alex, her hand out to him. "This place is important to you. I can sense that. I've been acting like it's no more special than the quick serve line at Burger Buddies. I'm sorry."

"I know." Without turning to look at her, he grabbed her hand. He held it tight, so tight Holly almost whimpered from the pain.

Alex didn't seem to notice, or if he did, maybe he just didn't care.

She saw his chest rise and fall. She heard his voice. At least she supposed it was his. The words sounded more like they came from the temple itself, from the stones and from the floor, from the pictures carved into the walls and the strange, flat figures painted on the altarpiece.

"It's part of your heritage," the voice said. "Part of the legacy of all the shape-shifters. It's what gives us life."

Startled, Holly took a step back.

Alex countered with a move of his own, one that brought him within inches of her. "It's something you will learn about," he said. His voice still sounded strange, but this time she knew it was Alex talking. She saw his mouth move. She felt the words vibrate through him. The sound was deep-pitched and as tormented as the agonized look she saw in Alex's eyes.

"Once you learn more about our heritage, then you'll know why this place is sacred," he said.

"If it's part of our heritage, why does it make me feel so creepy?" Holly asked. "It's like something happened here. Something not very nice."

Alex cocked his head. His eyes lit. She'd seen her math teacher look exactly like that when someone in the class finally understood what obtuse angles were all about. "Yes. You can feel it? That's good. That's very good. Tell me, Holly, what do you feel?"

Holly took a minute to collect her thoughts. She wasn't sure why, but she felt like this was a test. Like Alex was expecting her to give a certain answer—the right answer—and if she didn't . . .

The thought made the hairs on the back of Holly's neck stand on end.

She glanced around the room and even though there wasn't much she could see in the dark, she remembered how the temple looked when all the lights were on. "I know this isn't a big place," she began. "But tonight, it feels smaller than ever. It feels like the walls are right against my shoulders, waiting to close in on me. And the ceiling . . . the ceiling feels like it's only inches from my head. The floor . . ." Holly shifted her weight. In her good sneakers, she didn't make a sound.

"I know the floor is made of stone, but it feels soft and mushy." Holly shivered. "Like quicksand. It feels like there's something here," she said glancing around, afraid of what she might see. "Something I don't like. I saw you when I came in, Alex, you looked . . . you looked like you were praying. But this doesn't feel like a temple to me. It feels like a tomb."

"It could be." Finally, Alex let go of her hand. He walked around to the other side of the altar. "It could be a tomb," he said. "That's why I was praying to the goddess. You see, you're right. There is something here. Hidden in the temple. Something that could mean death to all the shape-shifters."

Goosebumps raced full blast up Holly's arms and into her shoulders. She wasn't usually afraid of the dark, but something in this place made it impossible not to be scared. She hurried across the room and took Alex's hands.

"Something hidden? What is it?"

She heard Alex haul in a long breath and let it out slowly. "An amulet," he explained. "A gold charm. It has great power over the shape-shifters. The Power of Life. The Power of Death. Many thousands of years ago, the amulet was hidden somewhere in the Temple of Bast, but we've never been able to find it. Will you help me, Holly? Will you help me look for it now?''

Holly was glad there were no lights on. If there were, she was certain Alex would see how skeptical she looked. From what she could remember of the temple, there wasn't much place in it to hide anything.

Four stone walls.

A stone floor.

A couple statues.

The altar slab.

''I don't see where it could be . . .''

Alex lifted her hands. She felt his lips brush the tips of her fingers, first of the right hand, then of the left. He stood there like that for a long time, her hands raised in his.

''Close your eyes,'' he said, ignoring her protest completely. ''Close your eyes and try to remember the last time we were here together.''

''But, Alex, we've never been—''

''I said, close your eyes and try to remember!'' Alex's patience snapped. His words slammed into Holly. She winced and pulled back, but Alex wasn't about to let go. His fingers gripping hers like a vise, he waited for the echo of his words to die down.

''Now close your eyes.'' His voice was soothing again. Hypnotic. But Holly could tell it took all his strength to keep his temper.

She closed her eyes.

The silence that surrounded them was as deep and heavy as the darkness.

Holly didn't hear a thing.

She couldn't see a thing.

Her mind was as blank as a freshly washed blackboard. There wasn't a trace of anything on it.

Then something happened.

A flash behind her eyes. Nothing more.

Holly let out a strangled sob.

She couldn't remember anything about this place. Not anything.

Except blood.

"No!" Holly's voice sounded small and frightened, like the cry of a lost animal. She tried to stop the memory, but she couldn't. She tried to hold back her tears, but that was impossible. She tried to tell herself that she was here, here at Los Gatos University where her dad worked, and she was Holly Callison, and she was with Alex Sarandon, and nothing in the past could touch her, nothing could hurt her.

"No!" She cried out again. Her eyes flew open. She jerked away from Alex.

He was beside her instantly, one arm wrapped around her shoulders. "Holly. Come on, let's—"

"No! Stay away from me. I don't want to remember. I don't want to find the amulet. It can hurt us, Alex. I don't want to know where it is."

"It's all right. Really." Alex sounded as soothing now as he had sounded angry just a couple moments ago. "We won't try that again. I promise. We'll try something different. Something that won't make you remember. Come on, let's just see if we can find the amulet. We won't try and figure out what your memories are all about, we'll just cast about with our minds and see if we can pick up on anything."

Holly nodded. Alex led her back to the altar and they sat down on the floor directly in front of it. He took her hand.

"Okay," he said. "Now just relax. Tell me. Do you feel anything?"

When Holly flinched, he held on tight. "That's not what I meant," he explained. "I mean, do you feel like the amulet might be here anywhere? I've tried to find it myself and it's impossible. I thought maybe if we combined both our powers—"

"Wait a minute!" Holly jiggled her shoulders. It felt like an icy hand was writing letters on her back. "I do feel something," she said. "Do you, Alex? It's here. Very close. I can see it in my mind. A beautiful charm in the shape of the goddess. It's—"

Holly's words froze on her lips when the light in the outside hallway snapped on.

It wasn't easy sitting here doing nothing when there was a human so near.

Alex signalled Holly to stay right where she was, in the deepest, darkest shadow behind the altar stone. Without moving more than an inch or two, he glanced around the altar.

Joe Pendergrast was out in the hallway, pacing back and forth in front of the open temple doors.

"Darn security system! I tell them over and over. But do they listen?" Joe shook his head vigorously. "That fancy new-fangled security system don't always show when these doors are left open. Sure it's supposed to. But it don't. They go away at closin' time''—he waved his hand vaguely toward the stair-way—''and they leave this crazy temple thing stand-in' wide open and nobody ever notices it on the security console. Ain't like back in the old days. That's for sure. Ain't like when we used to go around checkin' all the doors ourselves. Now they say, 'Let the security system do it.' But it don't always work, does it?''

Still pacing and mumbling, Joe stopped directly in front of the doorway. Though all the lights were on out in the hallway, the temple was pitch-black. Joe was an old man, terribly thin, and not too tall. Lit from behind, his silhouette reminded Alex of a scare-crow.

He snickered and looked at Holly. She was crouched down in the farthest corner of the temple, her eyes wide with fear.

''*It's a good thing we changed shapes as soon as we heard him coming.*'' Alex sent the message di-rectly into Holly's mind using the Gift. He was anx-ious to calm her down. ''*He'll never see us in the dark.*''

What a shame.

The idea was so sudden and delicious, it caused Alex's claws to tingle. If he was in his human form, he knew he'd be smiling. The feeling still tickling the corners of his mouth, he turned his attention back to Joe.

It was a shame Joe didn't have the guts to come into the temple. If he did, Alex would have the op-portunity to scare him senseless.

Alex's broad chest heaved.

It was a shame to be this close to a human and not to be able to do anything. To sit here like a frightened child, hiding in the dark. Yes. It was a shame Joe wasn't going to check out the temple.

Because if he did . . .

Electricity raced through Alex's veins.

If Joe did come in the room, Alex would be forced into action. He knew that. He'd have to do something—anything—to protect the secret of the panthers.

Alex's mouth watered. Every inch of his body prickled.

It had been too long since he'd tasted human blood.

8

The thought crept up on Alex and hit him like a two-ton truck.

He hadn't had any human blood since that night last fall when Mr. Tollifson had stumbled onto the existence of the panthers and Alex had to silence him. Forever.

The memory was still fresh in his mind, and Alex flicked his tongue over his canine teeth.

Even after all these months, he could almost taste the metallic flavor of Mr. Tollifson's blood. How hot it was in his mouth. How it coated his throat and made his stomach burn. How it danced through his veins, and sparkled through his body, and made his head and heart feel like they did in the old days, when he worshipped the goddess openly and all men recognized his power. Recognized it and feared it.

Joe was a lot skinnier than Mr. Tollifson. Alex could see that from here. And Joe was so old, Alex was certain his flesh would be stringy. But even so, it would be especially delicious to take a taste of Joe's blood.

Because he knew Joe was afraid.

And Alex hated fear.

It was the worst of all weaknesses.

He could sense the fear coming from Joe. He could see it. The old man bent at the waist and peeked into the room, the toes of his shoes dangling over some imaginary line separating the hallway from the temple.

"Come on. Just a little more."

Alex fixed his gaze on the old man and didn't look away.

"A couple of inches. That's all. A couple more inches and you'll be inside. Inside, where it's safe. Nothing will hurt you. Not in here."

Joe scraped his scrawny fingers through his gray hair and sniffed loudly, building his courage. He reached one arm into the temple and switched on the lights. He didn't come inside.

"Ain't no one here," he said to himself, craning his neck to look into every corner. "I knew it. Ain't nobody ever in here when I check. I should just get goin' back upstairs and—" Joe's conversation with himself trailed off into a series of mumbles.

"There could be someone here. You really should check. If someone was here . . . if you didn't find them . . . Doctor Callison wouldn't be too hard on you. But the university trustees . . . you know how they are. They wouldn't take kindly to finding out that someone was in the temple. And that you didn't check to make sure. They might even fire you and that wouldn't be fair, not when you're this close to collecting your pension."

Joe shuffled his feet, inching over the threshold. His left eye twitched. His gaze darted around the room.

"Ain't never seen anything as strange as this place." Joe looked around like he'd never been there before. "Crazy pictures on the walls. Weird altar. Makes you wonder what kind of things could go on in a place like this. Can't understand why they think it's art." He snorted. "Course some of that stuff upstairs, it ain't art, either. Spots of paint on canvas. No picture at all."

"The pictures on the altar aren't spots of paint. They're lovely. Haven't you ever looked at them? After all these years? Come closer, Joe. Take a look. You'll see beautiful pictures. Beautiful pictures of happy people. People taking offerings to their goddess."

Joe rubbed his chin. "I never did see those." With all of his attention suddenly trained on the pictures that were painted on the altar, Joe took a single step forward. "Funny, flat pictures." He took another step. "That's what they are. Funny and flat." Another step. "But they are kind of pretty."

"They're more than pretty. They're magic. Did you know that, Joe? Did you know that there's magic inside this temple? Just a little closer. A little closer to the altar, Joe. You'll feel the magic then. You'll see how pretty the pictures really are."

"Like they was painted with colors that make 'em glow from the inside." His eyes bright, his voice filled with excitement, Joe abandoned what was left of his caution. Hurrying to the altar, he knelt down on one knee and bent to study the pictures. "They're still happy, all these funny, flat people. Still happy after all these years.''

"That's right, Joe." The muscles in Alex's back legs tensed. He crouched, ready to spring. *"That's right. Just keep still and—"*

A snarl ripped through the stillness in the temple.

His face as white as his shirt, Joe jumped up. He stood stock-still, his arms out at his sides, his jaw slack.

Another, louder growl echoed through the room.

"Wh . . . wh . . . ?" Joe's eyes were as big as saucers. His breathing was so harsh, Holly could hear it even from where she crouched behind the altar. "Who's that? Who's there?" By this time, Joe was babbling like a baby.

Holly opened her jaws and let out a roar loud enough to wake the dead.

That was enough to get Joe moving.

He turned around and ran out of the temple and up the stairs as fast as he could.

Holly slipped around the corner and watched him go. She knew she should have felt guilty about scaring the old man. And she did. But what she felt more than anything was confused.

She couldn't believe what had just happened, even though she saw it with her own eyes and heard it— if not with her ears then at least in her head.

Alex had told Joe to check out the temple.

And Joe did.

Alex had suggested that he come inside.

And Joe did.

Alex had ordered Joe to look at the paintings on the altar, to kneel down so that it would be impossible for him to see the panther poised above him, ready to pounce.

And Joe did.

Without protest.

Without question.

Alex had controlled Joe's thoughts.

He'd controlled Joe's actions.

And Joe never knew it.

Holly was shaken out of her thoughts by the sound of laughter.

Her head came up. Alex was sitting on the altar. He was back in his human form, his arms wrapped around his knees. He was laughing like crazy.

"I can't believe it!" he said between gulps of air to steady himself. "I can't believe you had the guts! It's no wonder I love you, Holly, you're—"

"How could you do that?" As quick as she could, Holly changed, too. She stared at Alex, dumbfounded. "Why would you want to scare a nice old guy like Joe?"

"Me? Scare Joe?" Alex was the picture of innocence. "I'm not the one who growled. I'm not the one who made him run out of here like a bat out of—"

"But you were going to scare him, weren't you? You were waiting for him to get close enough and then you were going to pop out of somewhere and scare the daylights out of him. I couldn't let you do that. At least he only heard me. Someone's bound to convince him he was imagining the whole thing. But if he saw you—''

A sudden thought struck Holly. She looked over at the stairway. Her voice was quiet, thoughtful, as if talking through the puzzle would help her figure it out. ''How did you do that?'' she asked. ''How did you make Joe do what you wanted him to do? I heard you send the messages into his head. But that doesn't explain why he followed them. Alex, how did you do it?''

Still smiling, Alex hopped to his feet. He stretched, the motion as luxurious as a cat's. ''It's another one of the benefits of the Gift,'' he said, taking Holly's arm. ''And I'd love to explain it to you fully, but right now . . .'' He cocked his head and listened to the faint sounds of a commotion going on above their heads. His eyes never losing their sparkle, he tugged Holly toward the door and down the hall that led to the back stairway and the museum's service entrance. ''. . . I think our friend Joe has called the police,'' he said. ''We'll come back another night. Right now, it's time for us to get out of here.''

Holly just didn't get it.

If she and Laila were exactly the same height, why did it always seem like Laila was looking down her nose at her?

Like right now.

Laila was standing out in the hallway, blocking the way into the auditorium where play practice was about to begin. She was wearing the most gorgeous hand-knit sweater Holly had ever seen, a pair of slacks that looked like they were made just for her, and a pair of soft, buttery leather boots the same jet-black color as Laila's hair.

Her top lip curled when she saw Holly. "I suppose you're coming to the party?" Laila asked the question, but she looked like she didn't really want an answer. Or if she did, she looked like it better be the one she wanted it to be.

Holly wasn't at all sorry to disappoint her. She gave Laila her biggest, brightest smile. "If it's Alex's birthday party you're talking about, of course I'm coming," Holly said. "As a matter of fact, he said that if I wasn't able to make it the night of the fourteenth, you'd just have to change the date."

"Alex's party." Laila sniffed like she smelled something bad. She glanced at her friends, Amber and Lindsey, who were standing on either side of her. "And my birthday, too. Alex and I do share a birthday, you know. That's how it works with twins."

Amber and Lindsey giggled.

"I'm so happy for you." Holly wasn't in the mood for Laila's sarcastic humor. She almost said something rude back to her. Then she remembered that more than once Alex had asked her to be tolerant of his sister—for his sake.

"I hear the party's really going to be something." Holly did her best to keep her resentment just below the surface of her words. She also tried to contain her excitement. Alex had promised her that there was something great planned for the party, a special ritual all the shape-shifters shared on their birthdays.

But he hadn't told her what it was.

Maybe Holly could get Laila to tell?

"Alex says it's something we'll all enjoy," Holly said, trying to draw Laila out. "But he said you like it especially."

"Did he?" For the first time that afternoon, Laila actually looked pleased. "I didn't think he knew me that well." She laughed. "I do enjoy it," she said, offering Holly as much of a smile as Holly had ever gotten from her. Her smile quickly turned into a chuckle. It reminded Holly of the way the Wicked Witch of the West cackled in *The Wizard of Oz.*

"He hasn't told you what it is, has he?" Laila's voice was as sly as the look that suddenly flashed across her face. "He's been teasing you, telling you there's something planned but not telling you what it is. I wonder why. I wonder if he just wants to surprise you or if . . ."

Holly frowned. "Or if what?"

With an elegant little lift of her shoulders, Laila laughed. "Maybe my brother isn't as confident about your abilities as he pretends to be." She looked at the auditorium door like she could see right through it, like she could see Alex inside waiting to start rehearsal.

"Maybe," she said, "Alex isn't sure you can handle it."

"I can handle anything you can." Holly tossed a look at Laila and her two buddies. "I thought you knew that by now."

"Anything? I wonder." Laila's smile disappeared. She looked like she was thinking very hard. It wasn't something she was used to doing, and it made her eyes squinch up and her lips look all puckery like she just took a big bite of a lemon.

Whatever she was thinking, it must have been something good. After a couple seconds, she was all smiles again. "How much has Alex really told you?" she asked. The look in her eyes was as cunning as a cat's. "How much has he really said about how important birthdays are to all of us? About . . . about what happens each year when we get older?"

Holly didn't know what Laila was talking about. She didn't care. She didn't like being treated like a third-string player on a team of all-stars. She met Laila's look head-on.

"Alex told me everything," she said.

Holly sounded far more confident than she felt. Alex had told her everything about the Gift, she reminded herself. Why wouldn't he?

But if she knew everything there was to know, why did Laila look so smug? So amused?

Holly never had the chance to ask.

Before she could, Tisha came flying down the hallway. She tried to stop five feet or so from the door, but her slick-bottomed leather moccasins didn't give her much traction. She slid the rest of the way and came to a stop right in front of Holly.

Tisha didn't like Laila and she usually didn't say much in front of her. But today, she didn't seem to care that Laila was there with her friends. Tisha was as fidgety as a Mexican jumping bean on a hot side-walk. She was out of breath and her eyes were shining with excitement.

Or maybe it was fear.

"Did you guys hear what happened last night?" Tisha asked.

Baffled, they all stared back at her.

"Am I the only one around this place with ears?" Tisha threw her hands in the air. "I don't get it! You'd think the whole town would be talking about this by now. But nobody knows anything about it." Tisha turned to Holly. "I can't believe you don't know. Your dad works at the museum."

Holly didn't like the sound of this at all.

"I think I hear Jason calling for rehearsal to start," she said, lying. It was impossible to hear anything through the heavy doors that separated the hallway from the auditorium.

Tisha wasn't about to let her get away that easily. She launched right into her story. "It happened last night. At the museum." She lowered her voice and moved closer. "Joe Pendergrast, the night watchman? He heard it last night."

Now Holly was sure she didn't want to continue the conversation.

"I do hear Jason now," she said with a nervous laugh. "That was him calling for everybody to be on stage. We're doing the big Dracula and Camilla scene today. I'd better get in there, I'm—"

"Heard what?" Laila's green eyes were narrowed and there was a strange, suspicious look on her face.

She placed a hand on Tisha's sleeve and bent nearer to look right into her eyes. "What did Joe hear?"

Tisha made a gulping noise. Her words came out in a breathy whisper. "The Los Gatos panther!"

"Oh, please!" Laila couldn't control herself. Laughing, she stood up straight and tossed her head. On cue, Amber and Lindsey laughed, too.

Holly wasn't laughing. Her palms were starting to sweat. Her stomach was feeling like it felt that summer she went to Disney World with her mom and dad and they all rode Space Mountain five times in a row.

Tisha looked offended. She had obviously expected a very different reaction. "I'm not kidding," she said. "Joe even called the cops. Linda told me. You know, the sheriff's secretary? She told me the call came in right around eleven o'clock. I'm surprised you didn't see all the commotion on your way home." Tisha turned to Holly. "You must have been passing by the college right about then."

"Oh?"

The sound of the single syllable from Laila's lips made Holly's skin crawl.

Laila stepped back and looked Holly up and down. "You were near the museum about that time last night?"

Holly shrugged away the question. "I walked by on my way home," she said. "So what of it? I didn't see a thing. I didn't hear a thing. Guess I must have just missed all the excitement."

"Right." Laila's smile was as chilling as her voice. "I suppose my brother was with you?"

Holly didn't say a thing. She didn't have to. Tisha answered for her.

"Of course he was with her!" She rolled her eyes. "Do you think I'd let Holly walk home from my house that late at night all by herself? With panthers running around town?"

"Wait a minute!" It was Holly's turn to break in. She shook her head, trying to organize her thoughts. "How do you know?" she asked Tisha. "I left you at your house. Up in your room. How do you know I was with Alex?"

Tisha's face got red. She mumbled something incoherent.

Holly wasn't about to let her off the hook that easily. She stared hard at Tisha, waiting for the truth. "Tisha?"

Tisha chewed her lower lip. She looked up at Holly through the fringe of her dark bangs. "I followed you all the way to the museum," she said.

"Followed us?" Holly's voice was a squeak.

"Then you were there!" Laila exploded. She didn't give Tisha the chance to say any more. She pointed her index finger right at Holly and her voice dripped anger.

"You tell Count Dracula something. For me. Tell him there are certain . . ." She searched for the word. "Certain rules," she finally said. "Rules about power. And rules about using it. Rules about what you can and can't do without telling everyone in your pack." The look she gave Holly made it pretty clear she knew why they were at the museum last night. She knew they were looking for the amulet.

"Tell Alex that a violation of those rules would be disloyal. It would be a betrayal. If it's true . . ." This time, Laila couldn't find the right words. She gave up. "Well, just tell him we'll talk about it later."

With that, Laila stalked away.

Tisha watched her go, Amber and Lindsey trailing behind. "What's wrong with that girl?" She made a face at Laila's back. "If I knew that was the kind of reaction I was going to get, I wouldn't have even mentioned Joe and the panther. I guess I should know better. I never even would have said anything if I wasn't so worried about you, Holly."

"Worried? About me?" Holly forced a laugh. "Why would you worry about me? You already admitted you followed me until I met Alex. You knew I was in good hands."

Tisha looked away. "Yeah. I followed you all the way to the museum. But what I didn't say in front of Laila was that I didn't stop there." She looked up at Holly. Tisha's eyes were shimmering with tears, her voice was shaking with fright. "Holly, I saw you and Alex go into the museum."

9

"You what?"

Holly's hands were shaking as bad as Tisha's voice. Her pulse was pounding. Her head was spinning so fast, she wasn't sure she'd be able to hear Tisha's answer, but she asked the question anyway. "You saw us go into the museum?"

"Well . . ." One corner of Tisha's mouth twisted up. "Not exactly go in . . ."

"Not exactly." It was hard for Holly to talk. Her mouth was suddenly as dry as sand. "What exactly do you mean by 'not exactly'?"

"Well, I saw you guys walk over to the museum. And I saw you stand there for a while. Then you went around to the back and—"

"And?" Holly held her breath.

"And you didn't come out again. Not for a really long time." Tisha shrugged. "So I went around back to see what was up. You weren't back there, either." Tisha looked just as confused as she must have been last night. Still puzzled, she went over the whole thing again, step by step.

"I know they're working on that new science building behind the museum. The whole place is torn up and roped off because of the construction. You couldn't leave that way. You didn't come out the front way. And you couldn't go out the back way. The only place you could have gone was inside.'' Tisha's face was very serious. Her lower lip trembled.

"That's when I noticed there was a window open near the back door of the museum, over by the maintenance area. It's so high up on the wall, I don't know how you could get to it. But it was the only way you could have gotten in.'' Tisha gripped Holly's sleeve and held on tight.

"I always thought Alex was the kind of guy who'd do stuff for kicks, just to see if he could pull it off. That's one of the reasons I told you to stay away from him. He's dangerous. He's impulsive. Don't you see, Holly? He could get you in a lot of trouble. I don't care who your dad is. You guys could have been arrested for going into the museum like that. And if that's not enough to scare you, just think about Joe! He heard the panther last night, Holly. He swears he was down in that creepy old temple and it growled at him. The panther was in the museum!'' Tisha held onto Holly tighter than ever. Her voice cracked. "You were in the museum, too. Something awful could have happened!''

Holly closed her eyes and thanked her lucky stars. Tisha hadn't seen anything. Not really.

But Tisha was suspicious. And she was waiting for an explanation.

Holly scrambled to give her one. "It's supposed to be a secret,'' she said.

Just as Holly suspected, the hint of something mysterious made Tisha's eyes brighten. She looked at Holly eagerly. "Yes?"

"You see"—Holly lowered her voice to a whisper—"we knew the panther would be there."

"What?" Tisha looked like one of those characters in a cartoon whose face gets bright red and whose eyes bug out when it's surprised. She could barely contain herself. "You knew? About the panther?"

Holly nodded earnestly. "You're right about Alex," she said. "He is impulsive. That's because he's also very brave. You see, he was working with Mr. Tollifson on trapping the panther when—"

"Oh, Holly!" Tisha's voice was choked with tears. "That must have been so hard for Alex. You mean he was actually helping Tollifson? Helping him catch the panther? And nobody knew it? It must have been terrible for him when the panther—"

"It's not exactly like that." Holly couldn't bear to see Tisha suffer. "I told you last night, I don't think there is a panther. Mr. Tollifson didn't, either."

"But he was killed by something."

"Someone." Holly gave Tisha a meaningful look. She ignored the little voice of guilt that was already nibbling away at her conscience. As long as she was lying, she might as well make it really good. "We— Alex and I—we think there's someone trying to scare the people of Los Gatos. You know, by using the panther legend. It turns out that my dad agrees with us. Not only that, but Dad thinks this all might be tied into a shipment of valuable art the museum received not too long ago. There was something special in that shipment, something that this person wants. And he's using the legend to try and get it. Dad hasn't let us in on the whole thing, of course. He's being very secretive. Some of it I've been able to put together myself. I guess between Dad and the police, they've got a pretty good scheme cooked up to catch this guy. They—''

"The police? Oh, good!" By this time, Tisha was nodding, too, as if all the pieces to the puzzle were starting to fall into place. "I'm glad the police know."

"Yeah, me, too. Anyway," Holly continued, "Dad asked us to help him out last night. And, of course, we didn't get into the museum through that high window. Joe let us in through the back door. We didn't do anything heroic once we were inside. We waited in Dad's office while he patrolled the hallways with Joe. He said he needed us to sit by the phone, just in case."

"The phone." By now, Tisha was bobbing her head at every word Holly said. "Then you were the one who made the call! Linda said the person was so excited, she could hardly recognize the voice. Oh, Holly! And I thought you and Alex were getting into big trouble! You must think I'm a real idiot. How can you ever forgive me for thinking you were doing something wrong?"

"I don't need to forgive you." Holly squeezed Tisha's hand. But she wasn't about to let her off so easily. She pinned her with a look. "What I do need from you is a promise. You have to promise not to tell anybody about this, Tisha. You have to swear! Not a word to a soul. My dad would be furious if anyone found out. And we might be jeopardizing the whole investigation.''

Tisha crossed her heart. ''Promise,'' she said.

Holly wasn't through with her yet. ''And you have to promise never to follow me and Alex again. Never.''

This wasn't as easy for Tisha to do. ''But Holly, I could help. I—''

''Promise!''

''I've got the pennyroyal and the garlic and I—''

''Tisha, promise!''

Tisha's expression was positively painful. She looked up at Holly with a pathetic gleam of hope in her eyes. ''It's kind of like Panther Busters. It's pretty exciting and—''

''Tisha!''

''Oh, all right!'' Tisha moaned. ''I promise.''

''Good.'' Holly turned and punched open the door to the auditorium. She wondered how long it would take Tisha to realize her story had holes in it big enough to drive a truck through.

No matter, Holly told herself. She'd worry about that when the time came. She led the way into the auditorium. ''Come on,'' she said. ''Let's go see what's happening at rehearsal.''

Tisha followed without a word.

What Holly didn't see was that behind her back, Tisha had her fingers crossed.

• • •
Roses are red,
Violets are blue.
The Valentine's Day dance is pretty soon
and I know you're going with Alex, but
could I have one dance with you?

All right, so it's not much of a poem. Hey, who
said I was Shakespeare? (He did write poems,
didn't he?) Anyway, the Valentine's dance is in a
couple weeks. I wasn't going to go, but Tisha
talked me into it. She said I could tag along with
her and Zack. I know you'll be busy most of the eve-
ning, but if you could just spare a couple
minutes??? Please! One dance for old times' sake?

Holly read over the note she found stuck between
the pages of her script. As fast as she could, she
folded it and tucked it into her math book.

It was silly to feel guilty, she told herself. But she
couldn't help it.

She looked around to make sure Alex wasn't
watching, and breathed a sigh of relief.

Alex was nowhere to be seen, but Jason was. He
was on stage.

Holly sat back against the arm of one of the auditorium seats. It had been a long time since she paid
any attention to Jason. Too long. She'd forgotten how
much fun he could be.

Jason was busy being playwright, director, and producer. And he was having the time of his life!

He flashed across the stage to help some of the freshmen who had minor roles go over their lines. He helped the prop crew carry in a heavy table and a couple oversized chairs. He shouted directions to the lighting crew, did a sound check, and moved a big fake fern from one side of the stage to the other.

Though she didn't have the slightest notion why, Holly found herself sighing again.

It felt strange watching Jason's relaxed, comfortable moves. It felt . . .

Holly turned the thought over in her head.

It felt peaceful, she decided.

Jason wasn't nearly as drop-dead handsome as Alex.

It was as if some voice inside Holly's head reminded her of the fact.

She didn't need it.

Of course Jason wasn't as gorgeous as Alex. Nobody was. Jason had none of Alex's smoldering good looks, none of his devastating charm.

Jason was Jason, and she'd forgotten how tall he was, and how his blond hair glimmered in the light. She'd forgotten the cute little dimple in his chin. She hadn't realized how much she had missed his constant snacking.

As if he were reading her mind, Jason chose that exact moment to rip open a granola bar. He munched it thoughtfully, then crumpled the wrapper and tossed it, basketball style, into the nearest trash can. "Two points!" He gave himself the thumbs-up and got back to work.

This time, Holly found herself grinning.

She'd forgotten how content she felt when she was with Jason. He wasn't at all like Alex. Even though Alex told her they'd been destined for each other through all eternity—and Holly believed him—she didn't think it would be a comfortable eternity. Not with Alex.

There would always be an edge of danger with Alex. Always a bit of anxiety. It was like that extreme skiing Holly had seen on the cable TV sports channel. All out. To the max. No holds barred.

There was never any in-between with Alex. Never any time for her to just sit back and catch her breath. Holly thought back to one of the families she'd baby-sat for when she lived in Cleveland. The two older kids, both girls, were great. But the youngest in the family was a little boy named David, and every time Holly sat for him, she always swore she'd never go back again.

David was spoiled. David was stubborn. David was so full of mischief Holly couldn't even begin to keep up with him.

He was also the most gorgeous little kid Holly had ever seen. A face like an angel's. Holly frowned. And a personality that would make devils run for cover.

A lot like Alex.

The thought hit Holly unexpectedly. She swatted it away like it was a pesky mosquito, but it was too late. Like a mosquito, it had already stung her. It might not be right there at the front of her thoughts, but it was in the back of her mind, irritating and itching. And it wouldn't go away.

Fortunately, some minor crisis had broken out on stage while Holly was lost in her thoughts. There was a lot of yelling about missing wigs and misplaced costumes, a lot of running back and forth. The commotion diverted Holly's attention.

She looked up in time to see Jason handling the situation like a seasoned Broadway pro. By the time he was done, everyone was smiling again.

Jason must have felt Holly's eyes on him. He looked over at her and his face lit up like a Christmas tree.

''What do you say?'' He mouthed the words and pointed at her script. He obviously thought his note was still there.

''What?'' Holly pretended like she didn't understand.

''The dance!'' Jason put one hand in the air, one hand around an imaginary partner's waist, and did a couple of waltz steps. He pointed to Holly. He pointed to himself. He held up one finger. ''One dance?''

This time Holly couldn't pretend. Everyone in the auditorium knew exactly what Jason was talking about. They were all staring at her, waiting to see what she'd say.

''I'll talk to you later,'' she said. She hoped later was a long time coming.

It wasn't.

Jason hopped off the stage and came over to where Holly was sitting.

"So what do you say, fair Camilla?" He grinned. "One dance with the author, director, producer, and general gofer of this extravaganza? I promise. It'll be a night you'll remember forever!"

Holly laughed. But she knew she was only delaying the inevitable. "It's not that I don't want to . . ." She grimaced. She couldn't stand it. Even as she watched, all the excitement drained out of Jason's face. It was like watching all the air go out of a balloon. Pretty pathetic. "It's not like it wouldn't be fun, but . . ."

Jason pulled on his earlobe. "I get it. Your dance card is full."

"I'm not even sure what a dance card is." Holly tried to laugh but the sound fell flat. "It's not that." She forced herself to look up at Jason. She owed him that much.

"It's Alex's birthday," she said. She remembered the scene with Laila out in the hallway and added, "And Laila's, too."

"His birthday?" Jason scratched one hand through his hair. "Alex has birthdays?"

This time Holly's laugh was genuine. "Of course he has birthdays." She gave Jason a friendly punch on the arm. "Everybody has birthdays."

"Well, yeah, I know that. It's just that I figured Alex wasn't like the rest of us regular folks. He's so perfect, I didn't even think he was human!"

Holly's smile froze. So did her brain. She wasn't sure how long she sat like that. The next thing she knew, Jason was waving one hand in front of her face. "Earth to Holly! You in there?"

She snapped to attention. "They're having a big party," she blurted out. "Alex and Laila. They have a big party every year right on their birthday. It's the same night as the dance."

"So you won't be there at all?" Holly had to give Jason credit. He didn't even try to hide his disappointment. "I figured you'd at least show up," he admitted. "I mean, I figured you'd be at the dance and you might . . . we might . . . You know, one dance or something, but . . . hey, that's okay. I mean, I understand and all it's just that—" He broke off suddenly and looked at Holly in wonder.

"You mean Alex and Laila were born on Valentine's Day?"

It didn't seem that weird to Holly. Lots of people were born on holidays.

"Sure." She shrugged. "So?"

"Well, I can see Alex being born on Valentine's Day. But Laila?" Jason jiggled his shoulders. "She's got about as much heart as—"

"She doesn't have any heart at all."

Where Alex came from, Holly didn't know.

Suddenly, he was there. Right beside her. Joining in their conversation. And something told Holly he'd been somewhere very close all along, listening to everything she and Jason said.

Alex laughed at his own joke. "Laila's as heartless as they come," he said. He gave Holly a quick hug. It wasn't like he meant it. It was like he was picking up something at the Lost and Found, something he hadn't missed very much, but since it was his, he figured he might as well claim it. "But it will be a great party anyway." He was talking to Jason now, ignoring Holly completely. "Why don't you stop by? My folks hired a disc jockey. We'll be dancing there, too."

"I don't know." Jason had the good grace to look like he wasn't sure. Holly knew better. There was no way Jason would ever go to a party at Alex's, not when he knew Holly would be there with the guest of honor. "We'll see how the dance is going," he said. He gave Holly a wink. "My dance card might be full."

Was it Holly's imagination or did Alex's arm tighten around her when Jason winked?

She dismissed the thought with a toss of her head and pulled away from Alex. Her script rolled up in one hand, she hurried on stage and took her position for the opening of the big scene between Dracula and Camilla. Maybe if she could immerse herself in the play, she'd stop having such disturbing thoughts.

The plan worked. At least until Dracula made his entrance. Alex swooped in through the door of Camilla's bed chamber and leaned over her where she lay on the creaky iron bed Holly's mom had found in the attic when they moved into their house. Mom couldn't wait to get rid of it, and the Drama Club seemed like a worthy cause.

"For you." Playing his Dracula part, Alex swept Holly a low bow and handed her a folded piece of paper.

It was a single sheet torn from a spiral notebook.

On the front of it, he'd written "Holly Callison's Dance Card."

Holly looked at him in wonder.

Alex ignored Jason and the rest of the cast and crew who were waiting for him to say his lines. "They used them back in the days when gentlemen and ladies waltzed away the night in splendid country homes," he explained. "The young ladies would keep track of who they'd promised each of the dances to. Go ahead, see what yours says."

Holly flipped open the paper.

Inside, Alex had divided each side of the paper into ten or twelve lines. On every line he'd scrawled "Holly and Alex" in bloodred marker.

"Looks like your dance card is full." Alex dropped to one knee beside the bed and took Holly's hand. He looked deep into her eyes and lowered his voice to a whisper. "And it better stay full," he said. "Always. Always just for me."

"Happy birthday to you! Happy birthday to you . . ."

Holly sang as loud as everybody else gathered around the table in Laila and Alex's dining room. They'd already taken care of Laila—she'd insisted on being sung to first. Now it was Alex's turn.

All the lights in the room were out. The seventeen candles Laila had just blown out had been relit. They made a pool of brightness that illuminated Alex's face where he stood at the front of the crowd. He leaned forward slightly, his palms flat against the highly polished table.

The firelight threw odd shadows against Alex's face, shadows that flickered and wobbled as the candle flames danced. They caressed his jaw first, his cheekbones next. They skipped across his face, touching his lips, his eyes, the strand of night-black hair that tumbled over his forehead like a streak of drawing ink.

Alex's eyes sparkled with the reflection of the fire. He was smiling like a kid on Christmas morning.

The sight made Holly's breath catch in her throat.

Alex had promised her something special for tonight, but she couldn't imagine what could be any more special than this.

". . . Happy birthday to you!"

The song ended.

"Time to blow out the candles!" someone called.

"Time to make a wish!" somebody else told Alex. There was a smattering of applause.

"I know. I know." Alex held up his hands for silence. He looked around. The room was packed with kids. Most of them were dressed casually, but some of them still had on the formal clothes they'd worn to the Valentine's Day dance.

That just proved how popular Laila and Alex were, Holly told herself. A lot of people had left the dance early to come here, and a lot more had never given the dance a second thought once they had their invitation to this party.

Holly felt her heart swell.

It was a wonderful feeling standing here next to Alex, basking in the glow of his popularity.

It made her feel special. Beautiful.

"I want to thank you all for coming tonight," Alex began. "I—" He looked over at Laila and corrected himself. "*We* really appreciate it. I'd like to say a special thanks to Amber and Lindsey, Tom and Raymond." He looked at the other shape-shifters who were standing right across the table. "They're special friends and always will be. I'd also like to thank my sister."

This comment was met with a few nervous giggles.

"No. Really." Alex was still smiling. "You can't be a twin without someone to be a twin with, and if I had to pick, I would have picked Laila." He smiled over at his sister who beamed back at him like a mirror reflecting the sun. "We have our differences." He chuckled. "I guess everyone knows that. But we're more alike than we are different. It's great to have someone like her to share this special day with."

"Your frosting's going to melt!" Somebody pointed to where the candles were making waxy pools on the top of the cake.

Alex laughed. "Then I'd better talk fast." He slipped one arm around Holly's waist. "Last but certainly not least, I want to say thanks to this young lady." He gave her a squeeze and Holly felt her face blush. She wasn't sure if she was blushing with pride or embarrassment, she only knew that whatever the emotion was, it felt wonderful.

Her skin tingled where Alex's hand touched her. Her blood sang in her veins.

"You all know Holly and I have been dating since last fall," Alex said. "What you can't possibly know is how important she is to me."

He was still talking to everyone in the room, but he was looking only at Holly. He pivoted slightly so that he was standing right in front of her. He propped his free hand on her hip.

"She's my life," Alex said, his voice dropping to a rough whisper. "My world."

He kissed her.

Right there in front of most of the LGH junior class, half the seniors, and a whole bunch of people Holly didn't even know.

He kissed her.

And she didn't even care.

Holly felt like she'd soar all the way up to the ceiling like the colorful helium balloons that floated above their heads.

"Now for sure you're going to melt the cake!"

The reminder made Alex laugh. He pulled away from Holly and blew out the candles.

Everyone applauded.

"Know what I wished for?" Still smiling, he whispered in Holly's ear. "I wished we'd find that amulet. Soon. Then nothing could ever keep us apart."

Holly smiled back. She wished it, too.

She didn't have time to tell Alex. The next thing she knew, everyone was surging forward, wishing Alex and Laila a happy birthday, reaching for a piece of cake.

Holly left Alex to be the center of attention.

For the next half hour or so, she sat in the family room, listening to the great songs the disc jockey was playing, talking to just about everyone there. The Sarandons' family room was huge, three times as big as Holly's family room at home. The place was packed.

There were lots of familiar faces, and lots of new ones, too. But if Holly didn't know everyone before, she sure knew them now. Alex's speech—and especially his kiss—had shown everyone that Holly was important. And they treated her like she was.

By the time the disc jockey played the first slow song of the night, Holly was surrounded by friends, old and new. Ben Wiley, the LGH school newspaper editor, asked Holly to dance. She was all set to accept when Alex slid between them.

"Oh, no!" He gave Ben the kind of smile that Holly had learned no one could resist. Ben backed off instantly. "This dance is for me!"

Alex led Holly out to the middle of the floor.

She linked her hands around Alex's neck. He wrapped his arms around her waist. They swayed to the beat of the music.

After a couple seconds, Alex smiled down at her. Holly was all set to smile back, until she noticed that there was something more than just pleasure in Alex's eyes, something that made her skin prickle.

"Did you forget your promise?" he asked, his voice tight with anger.

"My promise?" Not sure what he was talking about, Holly gave him a questioning look.

Alex's expression never changed. His grip on her tightened. "It's disappointing to know you could forget so fast. Don't you remember? Your dance card is full. You promised you'd never dance with anyone else."

"Oh, that!" Holly laughed. Her laughter died when she realized Alex wasn't kidding. "Are you serious?"

Alex stopped dancing. He pulled away from her. "Of course I'm serious. But if you're not, maybe we just better forget this whole thing." He spun around, ready to stalk off the dance floor.

"Alex!" Holly tried to keep her voice down, but she was sure half the people in the room heard her. She felt a hundred eyes suddenly watching her. She saw Laila glide with Raymond, and she was sure Laila knew what was going on. She was smiling.

"Alex, I'm sorry." Holly didn't know what else to say. She didn't want to cause a scene. She didn't want to ruin the party. Tentatively, she touched Alex's sleeve. He didn't move away. He just stood there. Stiff as a statue. Cold as ice.

"I'm sorry." Holly's voice was so quiet, she was surprised he could hear it over the sound of the music. But Alex must have heard something: He turned his head a fraction of an inch.

Holly took that as a good sign. "I didn't realize you were serious."

Maybe it wasn't such a good sign. Now that Alex's face was turned toward her, Holly could see that he didn't look any happier than he had a couple minutes ago. His expression was still as dark as a storm cloud.

Holly looked down at her shoes. She felt like a kid who'd just been caught shoplifting a twenty-five-cent pack of gum. She was ashamed. She was miserable. And deep down inside, she knew she'd gotten into a whole lot of trouble over something that really wasn't very important.

That only made her feel worse.

Holly gulped down her humiliation. She decided to try a different strategy. "I was only going to dance with Ben," she said with a forced laugh. "I wasn't going to elope with him!"

"You were only going to let him hold you!" Alex's accusation slashed through the heavy silence that had enveloped the room.

Suddenly Holly realized the song was over. No one

was dancing anymore. They were all watching her and Alex.

Alex must have realized it, too. His spine stiffened. He tossed a quick, hard look at the disc jockey and another, harsher look at everyone who was standing around.

The disc jockey immediately put on another slow song and, after a few uncomfortable seconds, the guests fell into the easy rhythm of the dance.

"You were going to let Ben take you in his arms." As he spoke, Alex yanked Holly against him. His fingers dug into her skin. His eyes were only inches from hers. His lips were so close, she felt his angry words more than she heard them. "You were going to let him hold you."

"I wasn't. I—" Holly couldn't fight it anymore. There was too much authority in Alex's voice. Too much power in his eyes. She felt all her courage melt beneath the heat of Alex's touch and the fire in his eyes. "I never will," she said. "I promise. I never will again."

It was the best party ever.

At least that's what most people said on the way out.

It was the best party ever.

Holly looked up at the balloons that still hung near the ceiling like multicolored apples in a tree.

If only she could agree with them.

She looked over at the tables that were littered with cups and Coke cans and paper plates dotted with cake crumbs and smears of frosting. She looked at Alex who was lounging on the couch, his head back against the overstuffed pillows, a satisfied smile on his face.

"The cleaning service will get those in the morning," Alex told Holly when she started to pick up. He sat up and looked at the grandfather clock that stood in the corner of the living room. "We need to get out of here if we're going to have time for the rest of the festivities," he said, standing up and reaching for his jacket.

"Rest of the—" Holly started to ask what he was talking about, then stopped. The other shape-shifters were there, too, and they seemed to know exactly what Alex was talking about. She didn't want them to know that she didn't.

Not that she cared much.

Although Alex was acting like everything was back to normal, Holly couldn't forget the bitterness of their fight this evening. She was tired of pretending to be cheerful. Tired of acting like she and Alex were just as happy now as they had been earlier in the evening when he'd taken her in his arms and kissed her in front of all his guests. Right now, she couldn't think of anything more appealing than going home and crawling into bed.

Maybe a good night's sleep would help her forget their fight, she told herself. Maybe it would help her forget the fact that it wasn't the first fight they'd had, or that she and Alex seemed to be having an awful lot of fights lately.

Holly rubbed one hand over her eyes.

Maybe a good night's sleep would help erase the memory of the hard, disturbing look that had crossed Alex's face when he accused her of wanting to dance with Ben. Maybe it would make her forget that while they were arguing, she had been afraid.

Afraid of Alex.

Holly forced the thought out of her head.

The others had all grabbed their coats and followed Alex out the door. Automatically, she did, too.

Before Holly could get as far as the front door, the others had piled into Raymond's car. They were headed off down the street. Only Alex was waiting for her. He was standing near his car, casually tossing his keys in the air and catching them with one hand.

"Ready?" he asked.

"Sure." Holly shrugged into her coat and slid into the passenger seat. "Only you haven't told me where we're going."

Alex didn't answer her. He didn't say a thing. He started the car, wheeled out of the driveway, and headed for the outskirts of town.

Though his hands were steady on the wheel, Alex's eyes were bright with excitement.

And that's when Holly knew.

She knew exactly where they were going.

Even in heavy traffic, the ride to Harper's Mountain never took more than twenty minutes.

Tonight, it felt more like twenty hours.

The closer they got, the more nervous Holly felt.

It was like waiting for a math exam to start, she decided. Only worse.

By the time they were halfway there, she couldn't stand it anymore.

"Is this the birthday surprise you talked about?" Holly didn't know how jittery she really was until she heard her own voice.

Alex didn't answer right away. For a long time, Holly didn't think he would answer at all.

It wasn't until they stopped at a red light that he glanced her way. The pupils of his eyes were dilated so that she couldn't see any green at all. They looked deep and dark, like two black pools. His expression was rigid, almost like he was wearing a mask to hide his emotions.

"You can feel it, can't you?" Alex's voice was charged with all the excitement he didn't dare let show on his face. Holly knew why he hadn't said much up until now. He couldn't.

He was far too nervous.

"You can sense it in the air. Just like I can." Alex drew in an unsteady breath. "You can feel it in your blood."

"Yes." Holly realized it was true. Her head was buzzing. Her arms and legs were prickling. Her heart was pounding so hard, it felt like it would thump its way right out of her chest.

She wasn't sure who moved first, but before she knew it, Alex was holding her hand.

His touch should have helped steady her. Instead, his fingers closed over hers and she gasped.

Alex's hand was hot. His fingers tingled like there was electricity flowing through them.

The current stung Holly's hand.

It burned her skin.

But she couldn't let go.

She didn't even want to.

Holly could hardly control the feeling of excitement. The closer they got to Harper's Mountain, the more she felt it surging through her body.

Heat one second.

Icy cold the next.

Her stomach was fluttering like there was a whole pack of butterflies in there. Her breathing was so shallow, she sounded like she'd just run for miles.

By the time they pulled into the parking space next to Raymond's car, she was vibrating like a harp that had all its strings plucked at the same time.

Alex switched off the car lights and turned to Holly.

"Ready?"

"I'm not sure." Holly could barely speak. She pressed one hand to her heart. "I'm not sure if I'm ready. I'm not sure what to be ready for. I'm not sure if I should be happy, or nervous, or just plain scared."

Alex squeezed her hand. "There's nothing to be afraid of." He leaned nearer and looked deep into her eyes. Whatever he saw there, he liked. "You're ready," he said. And he smiled.

Alex got out of the car. He came around to the passenger side and opened Holly's door. As soon as her feet touched the ground, he changed into his panther shape. He sat back and watched Holly change into hers.

How different the world looked tonight!

Holly stretched and cast a slow glance around the parking lot.

When she was in her panther shape, her senses were always heightened. Her sight was crisp and clear. Her hearing was perfect. Her sense of smell was at its peak.

But tonight, nothing was clear. Everything looked a little fuzzy, a little off-center. She could still hear, but the sounds were dull, like she was wearing ear-muffs. Holly took a long drag of air. Her sense of smell seemed to be working just fine. Unfortunately, so did her sixth sense. A vague apprehension tickled her mind. A tiny voice inside her head told her to be careful.

Holly told the voice to shut up. She jiggled her shoulders and looked over to where Alex was sitting. Not that she needed to. She knew that while she was looking around, he was looking right at her. She could feel his eyes on her, like the heat of a flame.

He gave Holly a slow, lingering look. It was a look she'd learned to recognize, a look he sometimes used in his human shape, too.

When he looked at her that way, Holly didn't need to read his thoughts. She knew what he was thinking. The look said it all. It said he loved her. It said he needed her. It said she was his heart and his soul, his night and his day, his today and his tomorrow.

The look sent tremors up Holly's spine. It set her heart on fire.

Alex approached her slowly, each movement graceful as a dancer's, quiet as the night. *"It's my birthday,"* he said, using the Gift to speak directly to her mind. *"We have celebrated as humans. We've sung our foolish songs and danced our silly dances. Now it's time to celebrate in our true forms, to celebrate and honor the goddess."*

Alex looked over his shoulder, up toward Panther Hollow. Holly knew the other shape-shifters were already waiting there in their panther forms. She caught their scent on the wind.

Carefully, she watched Alex, waiting for his signal to join the others, sure that if he didn't give it soon, the anticipation and excitement would make her burst.

"Be patient." He looked at her and Holly knew he would have smiled if he could have. *"The night is long. We have all the time in the world."* He came a few steps closer, and she could see that his green cat's eyes were glowing with an excitement as intense as her own.

The next second, Alex lifted his head. His nostrils flared.

"Shape-shifters!" He called to them all and Holly felt the prick of their mental responses. They were waiting for Alex's command. *"Come!"* he told them. *"It's time for the hunt!"*

11

Alex dashed into the woods and Holly followed him.

She didn't stop to ask where they were going. She didn't stop to think about what they would do when they got there. All she knew was that Alex was leading. And she had to follow.

She was like a piece of metal being dragged around by a magnet. Or a moth that flies into a light whether it wants to or not.

She had no choice.

No matter what, she had to follow Alex.

When they got up to Panther Hollow, Holly saw that the other panthers were there waiting for them. They stood perfectly still while Alex passed. They waited until Holly ran by. Then they fell in step behind them.

Alex stayed at the head of the pack. Laila was somewhere on Holly's left. She could feel the jealousy and resentment that always seem to float around Laila like a storm cloud. Tom and Lindsey were in back of Holly. Raymond was over on her right with Amber close by.

"It's time for the hunt!"

Alex's words whirled through Holly's brain as she ran. She didn't know what they meant. She didn't care. She only knew that they stirred her blood. They made her heartbeat accelerate. They made her mouth water.

When Alex pulled to a stop, so did Holly and the rest of the panthers. They were in the tiny clearing that contained the ruined camp building where Holly had come looking for Tisha the night of the homecoming bonfire.

Alex signalled the others to wait. His steps smooth and silent, he made a slow circle of the building. Whatever he was looking for, he didn't find it. He came back to the front of the building, bounded up the rickety stairs and sniffed the air.

Just then, the moon came out from behind a cloud. Its light glimmered in Alex's eyes. It glinted against his teeth. It made his coat gleam like steel.

Holly caught her breath.

She knew now why she followed Alex without question. She knew why all the shape-shifters honored him as their leader.

As a human, Alex was smart. He was charming. He was strong and talented. He was gorgeous.

As a panther, he was all that. And more.

He was magical.

Automatically, Holly responded to Alex's mesmerizing power. She moved to leave the clearing when he signalled. She followed him, deeper and deeper into the woods.

Holly could have sworn Alex didn't say anything, not even using the Gift, yet she knew, finally, when it was time to stop. Without seeing the others do it, she knew when it was time to crouch down in the shadows. She knew when it was time to wait.

They sat that way for a very long time.

Holly listened to her heart pound out the seconds. She couldn't imagine where they were. Harper's Mountain wasn't very big, but it seemed like they'd been prowling through the woods for hours. Maybe they'd been going around in circles. Maybe they'd been up and down the mountain a few dozen times.

She wasn't sure anymore.

She wasn't sure of anything.

Her blood was buzzing with excitement. Her head was whirling. Her brain felt a lot like it did when she woke up from the disturbing dreams she'd had last fall.

Confused.

Cloudy.

Dizzy.

Until she wasn't sure if she was asleep or awake. If the images that floated past her eyes were real or illusion.

She could have sworn she saw Alex not ten feet in front of her. Or was it just a shadow? She could have sworn she heard the soft sounds of the other panthers breathing. Or was it just the whisper of the wind?

Holly shook her head, but she couldn't get rid of the weird feeling. She felt like she was looking at the world through a piece of plastic wrap. She could see everything. She could hear everything. She was aware of everything that was going on.

But nothing was clear. Everything she saw was a little out of focus. Every sound she heard was muffled.

Her thoughts weren't zipping through her head like they usually did. They were stomping around in slow motion. Like they were wearing heavy boots. And they were making her head throb.

Holly groaned. The sound came out more like a snarl.

She saw Alex dart her a warning look. She heard the others sniff their disapproval at her carelessness.

Then she saw why.

Up ahead, a deer broke out of the woods.

Every hair on Holly's body stood up straight. She held her breath.

The deer was a big, beautiful buck with antlers as tall and wide as any she had ever seen. Its eyes were brown and gentle. Holly knew that in the daylight its coat was brown, but in the moonlight it looked more like silver. It shimmered as the animal lifted its head to test the air.

Holly didn't know much about wild animals. But she knew they were downwind from the deer—the wind was blowing right in her face. The buck didn't catch their scent. It just lowered its head and nibbled contentedly on the grass.

What happened after that, Holly wasn't sure.

She saw Alex move, as quick as lightning.

She saw him leap.

She saw his razor-sharp claws rip into the deer. She heard the deer shriek in terror. When Alex moved away to circle around, preparing for another attack, she saw that the deer's neck was crisscrossed with bloody wounds.

No!

Holly leapt to her feet. She knew she couldn't use her human voice when she was in her panther shape, but she couldn't help herself. She tried to scream anyway.

No!

She tried to run forward, but her feet were suddenly as awkward as her brain. Her legs were stiff. Her steps felt heavy, like she was running through quicksand.

It didn't take long for the other panthers to rush past her and circle the buck. It lowered its antlers, trying to defend itself, but there were too many of them to fight off. With a deafening noise, the panthers were all over the deer, their claws slashing its silvery fur, their teeth tearing its flesh.

Holly's stomach lurched into her throat.

"Alex!" With all her skill, she screamed his name over and over, desperately calling to his mind with hers. *"Alex! What are you doing? Stop! Stop! Please! Alex!"*

It didn't do any good.

Alex ignored her. They all ignored her.

They kept up their attack. Alex faced the buck head on, dodging its dangerous antlers, dancing around its treacherous hooves, waiting for an opening when he could get close enough to use his teeth and claws. Laila and the others attacked from behind, charging at the poor thing again and again.

Holly stood frozen with horror. Her eyes filled with tears of desperation and disgust. Her breath strangled in her throat. She closed her eyes to block out the horrible scene in front of her, but nothing could stop the hideous sounds. The clearing echoed with the snarls of the panthers and the pitiful cries of the deer.

Finally, after what seemed like an eternity, the deer's screams got shriller. They tapered off with a heart-breaking moan. And then they stopped.

Holly opened her eyes. The deer had stopped fighting; its eyes rolled back in its head. With a gasp, the animal fell over on its side in the grass.

It wasn't dead.

Holly could see that it was still fighting for life. One agonizing breath after another.

As if its final, choking gasps were a signal of some kind, the panthers backed off. They sat down, their chests rising and falling to the pulse of their excitement and the rhythm of the deer's last breaths. Their claws were dark with blood. Their eyes were bright with pleasure.

Alex's eyes were brightest of all.

He stood over the buck and gazed at his fellow shape-shifters with a look that was nothing short of triumphant. Holly shivered. She was certain he would have been laughing if he could.

The thought made her blood run cold.

"Our birthday celebration!" Alex's eyes burned. A stream of blood dribbled from the corner of his mouth. Holly knew it wasn't his own.

"We dedicate ourselves to the goddess." His words echoed inside Holly's head. *"We dedicate our hunt to Bast. We offer her our sacrifice, the gift of blood."*

With that, he lowered his head and ripped out the deer's throat.

The other panthers roared their approval.

Alex looked up, basking in their admiration. There was a gleam of victory in his eyes, a scrap of bloody meat dangling from his jaws.

Holly was sure she was going to faint. Everything was out of focus before. Now the whole world started spinning.

"Holly! Holly!"

She was brought around by the sound of Alex calling her name.

By the time she could focus her eyes again, all the other panthers had gathered around the deer. They were ripping into it with their teeth, devouring the meat.

"Holly! Don't be shy. Don't hold back. Come closer. Holly!" Alex fixed his gaze on her and called to her again.

Holly couldn't resist. Not this time. Not even if she wanted to.

Like a sleepwalker, she crossed the clearing.

"Come on, Holly! Honor the goddess. Show Bast how you appreciate the wonderful Gift she's given you."

The grass was slick with the deer's blood. The nearer Holly got, the more she could smell it. The scent hung at the back of her throat. It made her teeth tingle.

Either Alex was reading her mind or he could see

what was happening to her. His eyes gleaming, he met her halfway.

"That's it." His voice sounded like a purr. *"Breathe deep, Don't be afraid. You think you won't like it, but you're wrong. Think back. Remember that night last fall? When you ate the steak from the refrigerator? You enjoyed that, didn't you? And that was old meat. Packaged. Not what the goddess intended for us."*

He lifted one of his paws. It was wet and dark with the deer's blood.

"Meat should be fresh. Blood should be hot."

He licked his paw.

"It should be shared."

He held his paw out to Holly.

Holly stared at him. She stared at his paw. She watched as he brought it closer. Slowly, he passed his paw under her nose.

Holly inhaled tentatively. The scent was intoxicating.

Slower still, Alex glided his paw around the edges of her mouth, until her fur was sticky and wet and drops of blood trickled onto her tongue.

Hesitantly, Holly flicked her tongue over her teeth. The scent of blood might be seductive, but it was nothing like the taste.

The taste was impossible to resist.

It made her feel like she did when Alex kissed her. Every inch of her was on fire. Every rational thought in her head disappeared. There was only one thing she wanted in all the world.

More blood.

Alex moved closer. He nuzzled her with his head, nudging her mouth open. His voice was the whisper of a lover. *"Not like that. Not a little lick. Take a good taste. A big taste. You'll see. Then you'll know how it feels. You'll know the pleasure. And the power."*

Again Alex nudged her, this time urging her over to where the deer lay in the grass. He roared, warning the others out of the way, and they moved, leaving a space for Holly to eat.

Alex stepped aside so Holly could get closer.

"My birthday gift to you," he said, with one look at the deer, one fiery look at Holly. *"A gift to bind us together. Forever."*

Forever.

Holly closed her eyes and let the word warm her insides. It reverberated through her head.

Forever.

And ever.

And ever.

Forever with Alex.

The thought was as thrilling as the taste of the deer's blood.

Holly opened her eyes, ready to step forward and join the feast.

Just as quickly, she stopped and blinked at the scene around her.

All night, the world had looked bleary, slightly out of focus. Now suddenly, everything looked different.

Holly didn't know why, but everything looked sharper. Clearer.

Like someone had taken a blurry TV picture and fiddled with it until it was as sharp as a knife blade, so clear, it hurt Holly's eyes.

She looked around. Every leaf of every tree stood out against the night sky. Every star above her head looked distinct, each one like a tiny piece of broken glass, pointed and deadly. Every detail of the scene in front of her was suddenly clear, like the horrible, sharp-edged visions of a nightmare.

In the center of a patch of grass that was dark and wet and sticky lay the body of the deer.

At least what was left of it.

Holly stared at the ravaged carcass in stunned disbelief.

The animal's eyes were wide open. They were filled with terror and pain. Its throat was completely gone. Somewhere in the middle of what used to be its neck was all that was left of its windpipe. It looked like a small, round piece of tubing, except that it was cut cleanly in half. Severed by Alex's teeth.

Holly shivered. She forced her gaze from the deer's head to its body.

The coat that had looked so silvery and warm in the moonlight was ripped to shreds now. It was speckled with blood. It was slick with saliva. There was a huge, ragged hole in the deer's left side. Holly could see its ribs sticking out. They were already stripped of their meat. She could see what was left of the deer's stomach. It was torn open and oozing something dark. She could see a glistening string of the deer's intestines, lying on the ground like a fat, white worm. She could see the deer's heart. Only minutes ago, it was pumping life through the magnificent animal. Now it was still. It was dead.

Holly's stomach turned upside down.

Only a few short minutes ago, the deer was alive. How ridiculously obvious that seemed. Yet now that the curious dizziness was gone from her head, now that the weird fogginess had cleared from her eyes, it was all so plain. All so frightening.

Only a little while ago, the deer was running through the woods, savoring its freedom and the crisp night air. Now it lay in a blood-spattered heap on the ground with the panthers all around it, like guests at a hideous banquet. Their heads were down. Their mouths were open. They were ripping the deer's still-warm flesh. They were licking its blood from their mouths.

She saw Raymond and Amber, side by side, sharing a portion of the deer's hind leg. She saw Tom and Lindsey, gorging themselves on something that was soft and fleshy. She saw Laila, feasting on raw meat.

Laila.

The most talented girl in school.

The prettiest girl in town.

For a second Holly wondered what all the boys who were head over heels in love with Laila would think of her if they saw her now, with her teeth in the body of a dead animal. With her face wet to the eyes with blood.

Holly swallowed hard.

She turned to where Alex was waiting for her.

He wasn't waiting anymore. With a movement that was almost a shrug, he showed her that he was tired of waiting. He sauntered over to the deer and, baring his teeth, he ripped a long strip of flesh from the body. He gulped it down the way big cats do, his head back, his tongue flicking in and out, his throat working so hard she could see the muscles moving.

He took another bite, but he didn't swallow it. His mouth full of meat, he looked at Holly, urging her closer.

With a sickening jolt, Holly recognized the look in Alex's eyes. It was a look she'd seen before. A look that glowed with pleasure and contentment. A look that simmered with excitement.

It was the same look he gave her when he kissed her.

The realization sent a wave of revulsion through Holly, a swell of disgust that started in her stomach and tore through her like a roller coaster at full speed.

"No!"

The panthers all looked up when Holly's voice rang through the woods.

They gave her a glance. That was all. They went back to eating.

Only Alex kept his eyes on her. He stepped toward her, a long tendril of slick red muscle and skin hanging from his mouth.

"No!"

She screamed the word. At him. At herself. And it

wasn't until it echoed back at her that she realized she'd changed into her human shape. She hadn't meant to. She hadn't tried. She didn't even know what she was doing. But she had changed, and she stood there in the middle of the carnage, her legs soaked to the ankles with blood.

"No!" she said again, her voice high with the beginnings of hysteria. "No goddess would demand this kind of sacrifice. Bast wouldn't ask us to kill. How can you find pleasure in this, Alex? How can you find pleasure in needless destruction?"

"Holly, relax." Holly couldn't help but notice that Alex didn't change. He stayed in his panther shape and sent her the message, all the while chewing over the ribbon of bloody flesh in his mouth. *"There's no reason to panic,"* he said, stepping forward, closing the gap between them. *"There's no reason to worry. You're a little upset. That's all. I understand. It's all so new to you. So exciting. Sometimes it's hard to handle. If you'll just come over here. Come closer, I—"*

"No!" Holly didn't wait for Alex to get any nearer. Screaming the word, she turned and ran into the woods as fast as she could.

Any second she thought she'd hear Alex behind her. Any second she knew he would outdistance her. He'd pass her by like she was standing still and close off the path of her escape. Any second she expected to feel the heat of his claws as he sprang at her from behind and brought her to the ground.

She didn't care. She didn't care about anything.

Off in the distance, she could hear the sounds of the panthers' feast. The farther she got from the scene of the kill, the fainter the noises were. But Holly could still hear them. Somehow, she knew she would be able to hear them forever. Awake or asleep, she was sure she'd never be able to forget the sounds.

The slobbery noise of the panthers' greedy chewing.

The frightening sounds of their satisfied purrs.

She stopped suddenly when she heard something that sounded more like a snarl. But she realized after a second or two that it had nothing to do with her. The sounds came from a long way off. The panthers were fighting with each other. Probably over some scrap of meat or a chip of bone. An awful, sour taste filled Holly's throat. She propped herself against a nearby tree and hung her head between her knees, waiting for the queasiness to pass. Even when it did, she didn't feel much better. Her head was pounding as hard as her heart. Her knees felt like they were made of rubber. And she knew, beyond the shadow of a doubt, that sooner or later—and probably sooner—she was going to throw up.

Holly pulled herself upright and headed downhill, picking up speed as she went.

It was a mistake.

Her knees were too wobbly to keep up the speed. Her eyes were too filled with tears for her to see where she was going. Her legs gave way and she tumbled down a rocky embankment.

• • •

Gingerly, Holly twisted her head from side to side.
Carefully, she flexed her arms and stretched her legs.

Nothing was broken.

All around her, she could see the faint outline of
trees against the sky, and not twenty feet downhill,
through a line of pines and scrubby bushes, she could
just make out the gray line of highway that led from
Harper's Mountain all the way back to town.

She had no idea how long she'd been unconscious.
No idea how late it was—or how early.

Holly dragged herself up to a sitting position. Her
stomach reeled. Every muscle in her body screamed
in protest. She would have liked to hop to her feet
and get out of there as quick as she could, but she
knew that was impossible. More than ever, her legs
felt like they were made of Jell-O.

She forced herself to sit for a few minutes and take
deep breaths. It didn't do a thing for her stomach, but
at least it helped the rest of her. Her head cleared a
little. Her legs felt a bit stronger.

With the help of a tree root that stuck out of the
embankment, Holly pulled herself to her feet. She
rested there for another couple minutes, straining her
ears for some sound that would tell her if the panthers
were nearby.

The woods were perfectly quiet.

Holly sniffed, testing the air for some sign of their
scent.

There was nothing.

Nothing but the night and the empty woods.

Holly slumped against the rocky incline. She

wasn't sure what to call the emotion that blocked her throat and made tears stream down her cheeks. Maybe it was relief. Maybe it was loneliness. Maybe it was just sadness, a sadness so deep, it felt like it rose up from the very bottom of her soul.

She didn't want to think about it. She couldn't. Not if she wanted to get out of here. Not if she didn't want to go crazy.

Taking a deep breath, Holly pushed off from the embankment and started toward the road.

It was slow going.

Her legs were shaking so much, she staggered from tree to tree. Her head hurt so bad, she had to stop a time or two and press her fingers against her temples.

But no matter how awful she felt, no matter how she told herself to concentrate on getting home—and nothing else—she couldn't stop thinking about what had happened tonight.

How could she forget the gruesome scene in the clearing, or the horribly mutilated body of the deer? How could she ever hope to forget the ravenous looks on the faces of all the panthers, or the fact that she'd felt the same powerful hunger? It surged through her body when she took that first taste of the deer's blood. How could she forget—how could she ever forget— the look on Alex's face the last time she saw him?

Holly shook her head, trying to get rid of the thought.

It didn't work.

No matter how hard she tried, she couldn't forget. In her head she still saw Alex sitting next to the dead deer, a long string of bloody meat hanging from his mouth.

In spite of how she tried to stop it, Holly felt her stomach lurch. She clamped one hand over her mouth.

She'd been right before, she decided, dropping to her knees.

No matter how hard she tried, it wasn't going to work. She was definitely going to throw up.

12

"You look awful!"

Tisha whirled into the room like a small tornado.

She whipped off her coat, threw it over the chair in front of Holly's vanity, and came over to the side of the bed.

"Your mom told me you got home from Alex's party really late last night. She said you didn't feel well." Tisha held one hand to Holly's forehead. It wasn't hot and for a second the concerned expression on her face brightened. Just as quickly, it was back again. She propped her fists on her hips and gave Holly one of those looks that said she was bound and determined to learn the truth.

"You don't feel well. That's an understatement if I ever heard one!" Tisha shook her head in disapproval. "You look like death warmed over."

Holly didn't say a thing. How could she?

Her eyes burned from crying. Her stomach muscles and her ribs ached from throwing up. It was no use even trying to fight the numbness in her brain. Each time she did, it only brought her face-to-face with the horrors of last night.

Without a word, she tugged her covers up to her nose and rolled over to face the wall.

"Well, just because you look dead doesn't mean you have to act dead." Tisha let out a puff of frustration. "I saw you yesterday afternoon. Remember? You were fine then. It doesn't take a rocket scientist to figure out that something must have happened last night. Something that upset you so much that you're pretending you're sick just so you can stay locked up in your room all day. Am I right?"

Nice try, Holly thought. But you won't get me to say a thing.

"All right, let's take the logic of this little argument one step further." Tisha cleared her throat. She sounded like she did that time she had to give a speech in front of the entire English class. "I talked to Ben Wiley this morning. He was at Alex's party last night. You probably saw him there. Anyway, he said you and Alex were as tight as can be. Laughing. Talking. Dancing close together. He did mention that you two had a fight over some dumb thing, but he said you patched it up before the party ended. So whatever it was that happened, it didn't happen at the party."

Another good guess.

Holly shut her eyes, but she couldn't shut out the sound of Tisha's voice.

"It happened after the party. Right? After everybody was gone. And just to prove that I didn't earn my reputation as the junior class know-it-all for nothing, let me take another guess. You and Alex broke up."

Holly's throat closed up with tears. She didn't want

to hear it. She didn't want to think about it. She just wanted to be left alone.

But Tisha didn't know that, and something told Holly even if she did, it wouldn't made a bit of difference. Tisha started to pace. As usual, she'd taken off her shoes and left them by the front door. Holly didn't have to see her to know it. She could hear Tisha's socks swishing against the plush, rose-colored carpet.

"That's it, isn't it?" Tisha's voice got more and more emotional as she convinced herself that her theory was true. "You guys broke up. No. I take it back. You wouldn't be nearly this upset if that was true. It wasn't mutual, was it? I mean, you guys didn't decide to part ways. Alex broke up with you, didn't he?" Tisha was surprised, then outraged. The more she thought about it, the madder she got.

"That rotten skunk! He's got a lot of nerve. I ought to go over there right now and give him a piece of my mind. Oh, I know what you're thinking. Don't bother. I can't spare one. But I'll tell you something, Holly. This makes me mad. This makes me really mad. I told you not to go out with him. I warned you. But would you listen? Oh, no! Not you! Well," Tisha snorted, "who can blame you? What girl could resist those green eyes? And he's got a body like one of those guys you see in those sexy magazine ads. Hunk. That's what Alex is. He's a hunk. He's a babe. He's the most horrible, terrible rat in the entire universe. Imagine him doing something like this to you!"

Holly heard Tisha pull to a stop next to the bed.

Tisha must have thrown her hands into the air, because now Holly heard them slap against her sides. "But hey," she said, "if you don't want to talk about it, just say so."

"I don't want to talk about it." Holly's voice was so hoarse, it sounded like a frog's croak.

"Right," Tisha grumbled with defeat. Her disappointment didn't last long. The next second, she was crowing with triumph. "Aha!" Tisha jumped up and down. "But you are talking, aren't you? That's a start at least. We can take it from here. You can tell me what happened. You'll feel a lot better once you get it off your chest. And I'll get all good and mad so I can stop over at the Sarandons on my way home and punch Alex in the nose."

Holly couldn't stand it anymore. She didn't know what was worse, lying here feeling miserable and sorry for herself, or listening to Tisha rant and rave. "We didn't break up," she said. "And there's nothing wrong with me. You know how my mom overreacts. She thinks every little sniffle is bubonic plague. And every time I feel queasy, she thinks I've got some incurable disease. I had a little too much pizza at the party last night. That's all. My stomach hasn't been able to settle down all day."

At least that much was true.

"Yeah, well . . ." Tisha didn't sound convinced.

Holly made a mental note to never underestimate the power of Tisha's curiosity. She could tell from the tone of Tisha's voice that she wasn't about to give up.

Her bed dipped and squeaked when Tisha perched herself on the edge of it. She heard a noise like Tisha was rummaging around in her pockets and another noise like she was ripping paper.

Tisha held a chocolate bar under Holly's nose and Holly's stomach did an instant upside-down flip.

"Want some?" Tisha sounded as innocent as can be.

"No!" Holly groaned. She didn't want to eat a candy bar. She didn't want to eat anything. During the long, sleepless night, she'd decided she would probably never be able to eat anything again as long as she lived.

Holly had to do something to get away from the smell of the chocolate. And she had to do it fast.

She turned away from the smell. But that meant she had to turn over. And that meant she was looking right at Tisha.

"I didn't think you would." Tisha had Holly's attention. That was obviously all that mattered. Pleased that her plan had worked, Tisha smiled like the Cheshire Cat in *Alice in Wonderland*. She tossed the candy bar in the wastepaper basket next to Holly's desk. "I borrowed the candy from Jason," she explained. "Told him it was for a good cause."

"It's not." Holly couldn't keep the misery out of her voice. She didn't even try. Her words came out like a moan. "I'm not a good cause. I'm a lost cause. So why don't you just go home and—"

"You're kidding, right?" Tisha gave Holly a searching look. She didn't like what she saw. Her mouth curved into a frown. Her shoulders drooped like she was carrying a heavy weight.

"I'm not sure what this is all about, Holly," Tisha said. Her voice was quiet and more serious than Holly had ever heard it. "But let me tell you something. Right here and now. I'll only say it once, but I'll say it loud and clear so you can understand. You may be ready to give up on yourself. But I'm not. Neither are any of your other friends. They—"

"I don't have any friends." Holly's words trembled with tears. "I thought I did. I was wrong."

"You have me," Tisha shot back at her. "But, of course, if that isn't good enough for you . . ." She brought her hand up to her nose and sniffed a little.

It was probably nothing more than a very convincing act, but in Holly's weakened state, she fell for it. "I'm sorry." She dragged one arm out from beneath the covers and patted Tisha's hand. "You are a good friend," she said and she realized that she meant it. "You always stick by me. No matter what."

Tisha's eyes lit up. "So you'll let me help you out this time?" she asked eagerly. "I mean, if this has something to do with the Los Gatos panther mystery—"

Holly didn't wait for her to finish. She bolted up and moved as far away from Tisha as she could. With her back against the headboard of the bed, she wrapped her arms around her knees. She was trying her best to look casual, but Holly wondered if Tisha could see her arms and legs trembling.

"What Los Gatos panther mystery are you talking

about?'' she asked, her voice a little too sharp. "And who says there's a mystery anyway? The only mystery around here is why you keep falling for all this nonsense about a panther. I—"

"Don't you remember?" Tisha leaned nearer and lowered her voice. "That mysterious shipment at the museum. The guy who's using the legend to try to fool everyone into believing in the panther. You're the one who told me about it, Holly."

"Oh. That." Holly picked at the edges of her blanket with nervous fingers. She had forgotten all about that crazy story she had told Tisha. She scrambled for a reply. "Don't *you* remember?" she countered. "We promised not to talk about it. Not ever again."

Tisha nodded, but Holly could tell from the look in her eyes that she had no intention of keeping that promise. She looked Holly up and down.

"If you're so sick," she asked, "why are you dressed?"

Holly hadn't even thought of it. She looked down and realized she was still wearing the clothes she'd pulled on last night when she came in. Dark blue jeans. An oversized green sweatshirt. A pair of her dad's sports socks.

The clothes she'd worn last night were bundled into a garbage bag and stuffed into the back of her closet. She'd take the bag to the curb herself on garbage pickup day, before her mom and dad had the chance to ask what was in it. She knew she had to throw the clothes away; she'd never get the bloodstains out of them. It was no use even trying. She'd never be able to wash away the blood, just like she'd never be able to forget the terrible slaughter she'd seen last night. Or the look of pleasure in Alex's eyes as he took part in it.

"I don't know what you're thinking, but I don't like it."

Tisha's voice jarred Holly out of her thoughts.

"You think you can hide your emotions pretty good, don't you?" Tisha asked. "Well, you can't. You can't tell me nothing's wrong. It's written all over your face, Holly. You're worried about something. Really worried. And I don't like it."

It wasn't Tisha's logic that brought Holly to tears. At least she didn't think so. It was the look in Tisha's eyes. The way her voice broke with emotion. The way she put out her hand for Holly to take hold of, like a lifeline thrown out to someone who's drowning.

Holly grabbed Tisha's hand and held on tight. "I can't explain," she said through her tears. "Not all of it. But . . . but I don't think I can see Alex anymore. I—"

Tisha's eyes popped open. "*You* want to break up with *him*? I never even thought of that!" Her surprise didn't last long. All the amazement drained out of her face along with all the color. "What happened?" she asked.

"N-nothing. Not really. Nothing I can tell you." Holly sniffed and wiped the back of her hand over her cheeks. Not that she thought it would do any good. Now that she'd started, she knew there was no way she could stop crying. "I wish I could, Tisha. I know you think you can help. But I can't tell you. You wouldn't understand. And even if you did . . .'' Holly's explanation dissolved into tears.

Tisha leaned forward. "You don't have to tell me if you don't want to," she said, giving Holly's hand a reassuring squeeze. "I guess all that matters is that it's important to you. Well, then it's important to me, too. I'll help you out, Holly. Any way I can." She hopped off the bed. "Hey! Jason is going to be thrilled to hear about this!"

"Tisha! Don't even say that. I'm not breaking up with Alex because of Jason. And I'm not looking for a new boyfriend."

"But Jason—"

"Jason." Holly bit her lower lip to keep it from trembling. "If Jason knew what I was really like—"

Tisha's eyes flashed. "Jason does know what you're really like. And he likes you. Not just because you're pretty or because you're a cheerleader or because you hang around with the right group of people. He likes you, Holly Callison. He likes the person you are."

Holly groaned. "No." She shook her head sadly. "No. You don't understand."

"You're the one who doesn't understand." Tisha obviously thought the problem was all but solved. She was smiling like her old self again. "And if you don't think I'm right, wait until you get to school on Monday. You should see what Jason did. You're not going to believe it!"

• • •

Tisha was right, Holly didn't believe it.

She stood in the center of the school gym and stared up at the ceiling.

> *Roses are red,*
> *Violets are blue.*
> *Holly Callison, don't you know,*
> *I'm crazy about you?*
> *Happy Valentine's Day!*

The banner was huge. It was hung up at the ceiling where nobody could miss it. It was decorated with frilly hearts and crazy-looking cupids with curly hair and gold-tipped arrows. It was written in letters at least a foot high. They were bright red.

Holly felt her face turn the same color.

"He's gone off the deep end," she said, still staring.

"I told you." Tisha shook her head slowly. She'd seen Jason's Valentine's Day message before and she couldn't believe it, either. "It was there when we came to the dance on Saturday. I think Jason was hoping you might show up. Nobody can figure out how he got it up there. I guess nobody can figure out how to get it down, either, or it wouldn't still be there."

"He's crazy." Holly couldn't help herself. She couldn't stop staring.

Neither could anyone else.

School hadn't even started yet and word about the banner had spread through the corridors. The kids who'd seen the sign at the dance dragged their friends in to show it to them. The kids who hadn't seen it couldn't wait. The gym was getting more crowded by the second, with kids looking at the sign, laughing good-naturedly, and pointing at Holly.

"I think I'm going to be sick." Holly wasn't kidding. After a whole miserable day in bed and another sleepless night, she wasn't feeling strong enough to put up with this. She pushed her way through the crowd, heading for the door.

And ran smack into Alex when she got there.

"Whoa! Careful!" Alex grabbed onto Holly's shoulders to keep her from falling. Even after he was sure she was okay, he didn't let go. Holly couldn't help but notice that his touch was warm and gentle. He was smiling.

Holly sucked in a painful breath.

Ever since she'd run out of the woods Saturday night, she'd been dreading this moment. And now that it was here, she wasn't at all sure what to do.

It would have been a lot easier if Alex didn't look like a million bucks. If his smile wasn't so warm. If his eyes weren't so tender. It would have been a lot easier if his touch wasn't sending Holly's heart into her throat and making her arms feel as hot as firecrackers where he was holding her.

"Are you all right?" Alex bent down and looked her in the eyes. "You look a little dazed."

"I'm fine." Even Holly knew she wasn't being at all convincing. She didn't sound fine. She sounded like a twelve-year-old girl stammering out her feelings to some boy she had a crush on. And she knew she didn't look fine. She'd seen herself in the mirror this morning. She knew how awful she looked.

There were dark smudges under her eyes from too little sleep. She was sure she'd already lost a couple pounds from being sick Saturday night and not eating a thing yesterday. Her cheekbones stuck out at funny angles. Her pants were slipping down her hips. She'd been in such a state of shock, she'd hardly paid any attention to what she wore to school today. She was afraid to even look. It was bound to be something that didn't match at all.

Holly didn't look fine at all and she knew it.

"I'm fine," she said, and she didn't even care if Alex knew she was lying. "I was in a hurry to get to my first class. That's all."

Alex chucked Holly under the chin with one finger and winked. "You don't have to be nervous," he told her. "It's all right. Really."

His voice was so gentle, his mood so cheerful, Holly wondered if she hadn't imagined the whole hunt and its bloody aftermath. Maybe it was just a nightmare.

How could she look at Alex now and think it was anything else? How could she look into his eyes and suppose she'd ever seen anything sinister there? How could she look at his lips and think of anything other than his kisses? How could she look at him and think how he looked with a piece of raw meat hanging from his mouth?

The thought sent a shiver up Holly's spine.

Luckily, Alex had already turned to talk to Tisha. She'd followed Holly to the door and was hanging around, just out of earshot, like a miniature guardian angel. "Could you excuse us for a couple minutes, Tisha?" He slipped one arm around Holly's shoulders and led her out into the corridor. "Holly will see you in biology."

"Sure." Tisha didn't look convinced. "If you need anything . . . ?" She gave Holly a meaningful look.

Holly smiled her appreciation.

"If you need anything . . . What's that supposed to mean?" Alex leaned against the nearest locker. He crossed his arms over his broad chest and tilted his head. He looked as pleasant as ever. There was a smile on his face, a sparkle in his eyes. But Holly couldn't help but notice that there was also a tiny note of danger in his voice. Or maybe she was imagining that, too.

Alex didn't look dangerous. He looked wonderful. "Does Tisha know something I don't know?" he asked.

"Of course not." Now that it came down to it, Holly couldn't make herself say the words she'd been practicing all yesterday. How could she? How could she look into Alex's eyes and tell him good-bye?

Alex was still smiling. "Look," he said, "I know there are some things we have to get straight. I understand you're confused. I understand you're upset. Our little celebration the other night—"

"Celebration!" Alex's insensitivity and the reminder of Saturday night's butchery was enough to make all of Holly's doubts disappear. What happened Saturday night wasn't a nightmare. It was real. All of it.

All of the horror.

All of the blood.

At the same time she fought to keep her stomach from rebelling again, Holly tried to keep her voice low. "How can you use a word like that?" she demanded. "How can you say that was a celebration? It wasn't, Alex. It was a murder. You destroyed that poor animal. Destroyed it for no good reason. How can you call something so ugly a celebration?"

Alex chuckled. "What's so wrong with what we did? Tell me, Holly. Hunters all over the world do it all the time."

Holly rejected his comparison with a shake of her shoulders. "That's different," she told him.

"Why? Why is it different?" Alex stood up straight. He was trying to keep his temper, but Holly could tell it wasn't going to hold for long. Already, he was rubbing the tips of his fingers against his wool sweater. "Most of the time, hunters kill for the pure pleasure of it. Their prey never has a chance. Not against high-powered rifles and high-tech tracking equipment. They don't even eat the meat. At least we feast on our kill."

"Don't stand there and tell me you got no pleasure from what you did, Alex. I don't believe it. I saw you. I saw the look in your eyes." Holly didn't realize she'd started to cry. Now a hot tear rolled down her cheek. Annoyed that she'd betrayed her emotions, she swiped it aside. "And don't tell me you're better than a hunter who goes out in the woods with a rifle. That's disgusting, too. At least hunters do what they do for sport. I don't think you did. I think you did it just to prove you were stronger than that poor deer. That you had the power to let it live, or to condemn it to death. What you did was for spite. It was for fun. I can't honor a goddess who demands the destruction of beautiful animals." She wouldn't be able to keep control of her emotions much longer. Holly was sure of that. Eager to get way from Alex, she spun around to leave.

Alex's hand clamped down on her arm. He whirled her to face him. All the hostility he had held in check was out in the open now. It burned in his eyes like the hottest fires of hell.

"Don't you ever question the goddess." His voice simmered like molten lava. He scowled at her for a minute, fighting to control himself. That one minute turned into two. Two stretched into three.

Finally, he drew in a deep breath. His jaw was rigid. His shoulders were tight with the effort of control. He didn't let go of his grip on Holly's arm. "I think you're just a little upset," he said, his words clipped between his clenched teeth. "I know I was the first time. All that blood can be very exciting. I understand."

"You don't understand!" Holly shook off his hand. She must have been talking louder than she meant to, because some of the kids who were walking past were staring at them. She noticed that Laila was standing across the hall, watching them carefully and enjoying the show. She had a huge smile on her face.

"You can't possibly understand," Holly said. "So maybe I'd better just come out and say it. I won't participate in that kind of thing, Alex. Not ever again. I don't want to be a part of your pack anymore."

Whatever reaction Holly expected, it wasn't the one she got. She was astounded when Alex started to laugh.

"You don't get it, do you?" he said. "This isn't some kind of sorority. It's not a club that you can walk away from. You're one of us, Holly. You have been for all time. You will be forever. You can't pretend you're not. You can't deny what you really are."

"Maybe not, but I can refuse to acknowledge it." Where Holly found the courage to tell Alex her decision, she didn't know. She squared her shoulders, looked him in the eye, and told him all the things she'd decided while she lay in bed yesterday. "I spent a lot of time thinking since the other night. Thinking about you. About us. I don't think I should see you anymore, Alex. I know that's going to be hard. But after next year, after we graduate, things will get better. I was planning on going away to college anyway. I'll just go away and never come back. That's all. I'll disappear somewhere. You'll never have to see me again. My folks will never have to know what I really am. It's the best decision. For all of us."

"And what happens on that wonderful day you meet some great guy and fall in love?" Alex's voice dripped with the kind of amusement that made Holly's skin crawl. "What are you going to tell him? I love you, sweetie, but remember never to get too close. If you do, I might be tempted to rip out your throat."

"I don't want to listen to any of this!" Holly screamed at him. She didn't care who was watching. The doors to the gym were still open and she bolted inside. It wasn't the fastest way to her homeroom, but at least it would get her away from Alex.

She knew Alex was right behind her. She could hear him breathing. At least for a couple seconds.

The next thing she knew, she heard him take a sharp breath of air. He stopped in his tracks.

"So that's what this is all about!"

Holly froze. She'd completely forgotten about Jason's sign.

She turned around. Alex was standing in the doorway, staring up at Jason's Valentine's message.

There wasn't any more amusement in Alex's voice. The smile was gone from his face. He looked from the sign to Holly and his face hardened with hate. "Now everything is clear. You won't get away with this, Holly. You can't possibly think you can choose Jason over me and—"

"I haven't chosen Jason. I haven't chosen anyone." Holly looked Alex in the eye. "I didn't ask him to put that thing there," she said, pointing to the banner. "I didn't know anything about it. If you don't believe that, then you don't know anything about me."

"I know all I need to know." Alex looked down

at her, his eyes dark with anger and pain. "I know I can't depend on your loyalty anymore. And that breaks my heart."

With that, he turned around and stalked away.

Through a haze of tears, Holly watched him go. For one instant, she thought about following Alex. She wanted to make sure he understood that her decision had nothing to do with Jason. She wanted to tell him it had everything to do with her. With how she felt. With how she thought. With how much respect she had for herself.

She wanted to reassure Alex.

She wanted more than anything to tell him she still loved him.

But she couldn't.

Holly's shoulders slumped.

She knew she couldn't tell him. Not today. Not ever.

Holly turned to cross the gym and head out the doors on the other side. Before she got that far, Laila was there waiting for her.

"I almost feel sorry for you." Laila didn't look sorry. She looked as content as a cat that just had its whiskers in a bowl of cream.

"Don't." It was nuts to feel so miserable and sound so angry, but Holly did. She snapped at Laila, "Don't ever feel sorry for me. I don't need your sympathy. And I don't need your interference. Why don't you go talk to Alex instead? He's the one who could use some of your tender consolation."

"Oh, I'll get to him soon enough." Laila leaned

against the door. She was blocking Holly's way and it looked like nothing short of a good, hard push would get her to move.

Holly was just considering it when Laila stood up and smiled. "He hasn't really told you everything, has he?" she asked, looking back the way Alex went. "I mean, I know you said he did. And I think you think it's true. Shame on Alex! He hasn't told you the truth. And you've been lying to yourself if you think he has. You haven't figured any of it out yet, have you? I mean about our birthdays."

Holly would have liked to pretend she didn't care what Laila was talking about. She couldn't. It wasn't the first time Laila had tried to tempt her with similar information, but for the first time, Holly realized it was something important. Something she needed to hear whether she wanted to or not. "What are you talking about?" she asked.

Laila's smile got sleeker and more satisfied. "I couldn't help overhearing your conversation," she explained. "Oh, don't worry. I doubt if anyone else did. You were pretty careful about keeping your voices down. But I do have . . . special abilities, don't I?" She giggled. "I mean, I had to strain my ears a little, but after I blocked out the background noise, I could hear what you and Alex were talking about. You said you were going to reject your heritage. That you were going to control your shape-shifting. That's when I realized that Alex really hasn't been playing fair with you."

Sometime while Laila was talking, a curious buzzing had started in Holly's head. She felt cold, like she was freezing from the inside out. Her stomach wobbled. Her heart pounded so hard she could hear the blood rushing inside her head.

"Get to the point," Holly said, managing to hide her apprehension behind something that sounded like anger. "You've either got something to tell me or you don't. And I don't have time for your games."

"Oh, it isn't a game." Laila smoothed her ink-black hair over one shoulder. "It will never be a game. You see, Holly, that's why birthdays are so important to us. The older we get, the hungrier we get. All of us. All the shape-shifters. It will happen to you, too. Wait, you'll see. By your next birthday, you'll be out in the woods hunting deer, too. Nothing can change that. You won't be able to help yourself. You'll have to have blood. More and more every year. And by the time you're an adult . . ." The light glinted against Laila's canine teeth. "By the time you're twenty-one, deer won't be enough. Not nearly enough. Nothing's going to satisfy you. Nothing except human blood."

13

Holly wasn't sure how she made it through the next couple weeks.

She went to school every day, and to cheerleading practice, and to play rehearsal.

But she had no idea what was going on.

She didn't even try to pretend.

She went through the motions, like in a dream, and forced herself not to think of anything at all. Because if she did, she was sure she'd think about Laila's prediction.

She avoided Jason because she couldn't stand the thought that he might look at her and know what she really was. She avoided Tisha because she knew if anyone could break her down and get her to talk, it would be Tisha. And she couldn't risk that.

She avoided Alex—especially Alex—because there was still so much pain in his eyes, and because every time she looked at him all she could see was the image of a panther, the killer she was destined to become.

None of it was easy. Holly had learned to be downright rude to Tisha. It was the only thing that put her off. She'd perfected the art of acting snobby when Jason was around. It made him self-conscious and shy and that was the best way to get him to keep his distance.

She wasn't nearly as good at pretending with Alex.

Because they were on stage together for practically the entire play, it was especially hard to avoid Alex during play practice. She wondered if he realized that every time Dracula came near Camilla, she felt like she would faint. She wondered if he knew that every time he touched her, she shivered with regret. And loneliness. And revulsion.

Besides what was written in the script, Alex hadn't spoken a word to her since the day he saw Jason's banner hanging in the gym. Once during biology class, Holly felt his mind probing hers. It happened again a couple days later while she was cheering at the final basketball game of the season. She knew he was trying to send a message, and she was pretty sure she knew what that message was.

He wanted her back.

More than anything, he wanted her back.

Holly pressed her knuckles to her lips, stifling a sob.

She wasn't sure how she did it, but every time she felt Alex's mind against hers, she raised her shields to keep him out. She had to. It would hurt too much to hear what he had to say, to know how miserable he was. Not only that, but she knew that if she heard him pleading, she might be tempted to listen.

Holly groaned. She rubbed her eyes with her fists.

It hurt.

All of it hurt.

And she didn't understand any of it.

Stretching, Holly got up from where she'd been sitting next to Bast's altar in the basement temple of the art museum.

There was no use trying anymore right now. There was no way she was going to find the amulet tonight. She would never find it, she told herself, not if she didn't concentrate more. Not if she kept letting thoughts of Jason and Tisha and Alex interrupt her.

"You done for tonight?"

Holly gasped and twirled around. Joe Pendergrast, the security guard, was standing in the doorway.

"Your pop told me you was down here." His eyes wide and uncertain, Joe peered into the temple like he expected to see something hideous there. "Don't seem a good idea for you to be here alone, but he says you'll be all right. Says you been hangin' out here for the last couple weeks." Joe shook his shoulders. "Can't understand why anyone would want to do that."

"It's not such a bad place." Even though she didn't believe it, it was the only reason Holly could think of. "Hardly anybody ever comes down here. And it's awfully quiet."

"Yeah. Too quiet." Joe danced around in the doorway like the floor was hot. "Don't this place give you the willies?"

It sure did.

Holly looked around the temple.

Joe didn't know how right he was. The place gave her the creeps. But how could she tell that to Joe or to anyone else? How could she explain that even though the temple terrified her, she had to come here? Ever since the night of Alex's birthday, she'd felt the place calling to her, drawing her like a magnet. She'd come here every day since then to try to find the amulet Alex talked about, not because he wanted her to, but because in her heart she prayed that it was the key to solving her problem.

"Gives me the willies." Obviously Joe hadn't noticed how preoccupied Holly was. He picked up the conversation right where he left off. He looked around the temple. "Your dad ain't told you what happened here a couple weeks ago?"

Holly shrugged. "Dad didn't say anything," she told him. It was the truth. Her dad hadn't said a thing about Joe's encounter with the panther. "But Tisha, my friend at school, she heard what happened. Do you believe in the panther, Joe?"

Joe didn't have to think about his answer for long. "Never did before," he said. "Oh, I admit, I always knew this place was weird. Sort of unhealthy, if you know what I mean. But I never figured it had anything to do with that crazy panther legend. Been hearin' that story since I was a kid. Never heard nobody connect it nohow with this place. Always just thought this place was strange cause of all them pagan Egyptian gods that used to be worshipped here. You know, Bast and Re and Sekhmet."

"Bast and Re and Sekhmet." Holly repeated the names in a whisper. She had heard Alex use them once. During the ceremony that made her a part of

his pack. "Do you know about things like that, Joe?"
she asked. "About the Egyptian gods, I mean?"

Now that she had him talking, Joe was finally more
at ease. He stepped all the way into the temple.
"Never did before," he admitted. "Not until that
night a few weeks ago when the . . . the . . . well, the
you-know-what was here." He looked over his shoulder and checked the corners of the room one more
time.

"After that, I got to thinkin'. You know, I was out
there a long time." He stabbed one thumb over his
shoulder. "In the hallway. I was kinda talkin' to myself and wonderin' why these doors is always open
when they shouldn't be. I never heard that critter
make a peep 'til I went over there. About where you
are." Joe came over to where Holly was standing. He
bent down and looked at the altar stone, just like he'd
done the night Holly and Alex were hiding on the
other side of it.

"I just hunkered down to see them pictures," he
said, pointing to the carvings. "And that's when I
heard it." He straightened and shook his head. "Like
I said, it got me thinkin' that maybe—just maybe—
that panther had somethin' to do with this place. With
these here Egyptians. Your pop said the idea was just
plain crazy, but he let me look through some of his
books. They didn't tell me nothin'. Then I had a
downright brilliant idea. I remembered there was
boxes up in the attic. Stuff nobody's bothered to look
at for the last fifty years or so. I went up and found
the papers that ol' Henry Cory Clare left to the mu-

seum. The diaries he kept when he was diggin' up this old place. I been doin' a little research of my own ever since.''

''Research.'' The word made Holly shudder. She told herself that in years of exploration, art history professors, anthropologists, and archaeologists had never discovered anything significant about the temple. It was unlikely a security guard had found anything important in just a couple weeks. Still, Joe looked remarkably pleased with himself.

Holly's hands started to shake. Something told her she should get out of here as fast as she could. But something else told her that she had to find out what Joe was talking about. She waited for more.

''Yep.'' Joe hitched his thumbs in his belt. ''Been readin' stuff I bet your pop never even saw. Old. Dusty. Whole stack of it. Nobody's bothered with it for ages. So nobody knows.''

''Knows what?''

''Why, about them gods,'' Joe said matter-of-factly. He sounded like he'd been an Egyptian scholar for years instead of weeks. ''About Bast. She's the cat goddess, you know. And Sekhmet. Funny name. That's the lion goddess. Then there's that Amon-Re fellow, king of the gods.''

Bast, goddess of the cat. Sekhmet, the lion goddess. Amon-Re, king of the gods.

The words of the shape-shifting ceremony whirled through Holly's head.

''And what did you find out?'' she asked. Her mouth felt dry. Her hands were shaking so bad, she had to stuff them into her pockets. "I mean, about Bast and Sekhmet and Re. What do they have to do with this place? And what do they have to do with the panther?"

"It's like this," Joe said. He leaned nearer. "Them gods are—"

A noise out in the hallway cut Joe short.

Joe bolted up, straight as an arrow, stiff as stone. He didn't turn around. He didn't budge a muscle. Only his eyes moved. They shifted back and forth and sweat broke out on his forehead.

"Who's there?" he called. When there was no answer, Joe tried again. "It's closin' time soon," he said. He tried to sound tough, but his voice was jiggling like a bowl of pudding. "You'll have to be movin' along."

Still, no one answered.

Holly looked out at the little bit of hallway she could see from where she stood. There wasn't anybody there, but she could have sworn she saw a movement behind the temple doors. They were propped open like they always were during the museum's operating hours. She knew there was just enough room between the doors and the outside walls for someone to hide.

"I'll check it, Joe," Holly whispered, so the person out in the hall couldn't hear. She thought she knew who was there and, if she was right, she knew it would be better—and safer—for her to find Alex than it would be for Joe. In a flash, Holly was out in the hallway. She reached around the temple door, grabbed onto someone's arm, and pulled.

"Tisha!"

Holly stared at Tisha, who at least had the good sense to look embarrassed.

"What are you doing here?" she demanded.

Tisha looked past Holly, scanning the paintings that hung up and down the hall. "Culture," she said with a guilty giggle. "Just here for some culture. You know, Monet, Picasso. All those guys."

Holly let go of Tisha's arm. "There aren't any Monet or Picasso paintings in this whole place," she said, grateful that for once she'd actually listened to something her dad said about the museum so she could catch Tisha in her lie. "You followed me, Tisha. After you promised not to."

Tisha stuck out her lower lip. "All's fair when you're trying to find out why your best friend has turned into the grumpiest, hardest-to-get-along-with, most disagreeable person in the whole world. Especially now that I know Joe's on to something."

Before Holly could stop her, Tisha zipped into the temple. Joe was so relieved to see it was a person, and not the Los Gatos panther, that he was grinning from ear to ear.

"This is great stuff, Joe." Tisha didn't bother to introduce herself. She slung her backpack on the altar and hopped around in front of Joe, too excited to keep still. "I mean all this stuff about the panther and what it might have to do with the museum. It proves Holly's original theory. You know, the one about that valuable shipment of art objects that came through here a couple months ago.''

''Shipment?'' Joe pulled on his earlobe. It was obvious he was thinking very hard.

''You know.'' Tisha poked him in the ribs and winked. ''That mysterious delivery. The one someone's after.''

Joe shook his head. ''Ain't had a shipment of anythin' in here for at least a year,'' he said. ''No money in the budget. That's what the college trustees say. That's why Holly's pop was hired. Get some money rollin' into this place.''

''No shipment!'' Tisha's mouth dropped open. She looked over at Holly and Holly could see the light of truth dawn in her eyes. ''You lied to me!'' Tisha stomped her foot. ''You told me there was some sort of conspiracy to steal something from the museum. You said—''

Tisha's words were interrupted by a growl that echoed through the temple.

''Did you hear that?'' Tisha grabbed onto Holly's sleeve. She didn't look nearly as scared as Joe. Joe looked like he was about to have a heart attack. Tisha looked excited.

''Did you hear that?'' she asked again, giving Holly's arm a shake. ''It's the panther. Holly, this is great! We've got proof! We've finally got proof!''

''What are you talking about?'' Holly tried to laugh off the whole thing. Her laughter fell dead against the sudden heaviness that filled the air. ''There's nothing here,'' she said, a little too quick and loud. She darted a glance around the temple.

No sign of Alex. But she knew he was here. She could feel the brush of his mind on hers.

Holly did the only thing she could think of. She tugged Tisha toward the door. "Nothing here at all. Why don't we just go upstairs and—"

It was all Holly had a chance to say. The lights went out. The world went black. And all Holly could hear was the bone-chilling sound of Tisha's screams.

"Tisha!"

Holly bolted up, screaming Tisha's name.

She opened her eyes.

She was in her room. In her bed. The sun was streaming through her window the way it did every morning right about seven o'clock.

"Tisha?"

Not sure what she was looking for, Holly peered around the room. Everything was the same as it always was.

Her backpack was in the corner where she always left it. The clothes she'd worn to school yesterday were folded neatly on the rocking chair in the corner.

"This isn't possible." Holly jumped out of bed. She went over to the rocking chair and grabbed her jeans and her green sweater. "Not possible," she mumbled. "None of it. I was at the museum. I know I was. I was wearing this stuff, and Tisha and Joe were there, and—"

The sudden memory of the panther's roar made Holly's throat close with fright. She pressed a hand to her mouth, fighting to control herself.

"Call her. Just call her."

Holly talked to herself like you might talk to a little kid who was afraid of the dark.

"She'll be there," she told herself. "That'll prove it. It was all a dream. That's all."

Her hands were trembling so bad, Holly could barely pick up the phone.

Instead of a dial tone, she heard her dad's voice. He must have been talking on the phone in the kitchen.

"Are you sure?" Dad didn't sound like himself. He sounded like he'd just had all the wind knocked out of him. "Right there? In the museum?"

"That's right, Doctor Callison." The voice on the other end of the phone sounded serious and very official. "The guard called in a little while ago. Said he found it when he checked the basement this morning. No identification on the body yet. If you could just come down to the station . . ."

The phone slipped out of Holly's hands. She caught it just before it slammed on the floor and carefully set it back on the cradle so Dad wouldn't know she was listening.

Body?

Holly was shaking so bad, she had to wrap her arms around herself.

A body? In the museum?

Holly's shock melted into hysteria. She ripped off her nightgown and pulled on her clothes. She was out the door in less than a minute.

She ran all the way to Tisha's house.

• • •

There was no one home.

Holly pounded on Tisha's door until her knuckles were raw.

But no one answered.

Sobbing, she sank down on the porch and held her head in her hands.

No one home. No one here. Body in the museum.

Shrieking with frustration, Holly pulled herself to her feet. There was one other place she could check, she reminded herself. One other place she could go.

Her muscles protesting every step, Holly raced over to Tisha's grandmother's store.

CLOSED.

Holly slammed her fist against the door where the little plastic sign hung. Whirling around, she leaned her back against the window. She had to calm down. She had to think.

Though her mind was working a thousand miles a minute, Holly forced herself to say her thoughts out loud. Maybe if she could just slow down, she'd come up with some logical answers. "Tisha's not home," she told herself. "She's not here at the store, even though the store's usually open by now. She's got to be at school. Yeah!" Holly face split with a smile. She congratulated herself. "That's it!" she said. "School. Tisha's at school."

She sprinted across town toward Los Gatos High, all the while repeating to herself, "Tisha's at school. Tisha's at school."

It was a great theory.

If only she could get herself to believe it.

Because no matter how hard Holly tried, she couldn't forget that she'd heard a panther roar in the temple last night. She'd heard Tisha scream.

And now there was a body in the museum.

And she couldn't find Tisha anywhere.

14

Holly ripped into Tisha's homeroom ready to corner the first person she found.

It was Jason.

Unfortunately, she wasn't prepared for the way he looked. She stopped dead in her tracks right inside the door.

"Good morning, Camilla old bean!" Jason saluted her with what looked like a riding crop. He was dressed in baggy tan shorts and a light-colored shirt. He was wearing a floppy hat, sunglasses, and knee-socks that didn't quite make it all the way up his bony shins.

"What d'you think?" Jason grinned and swiveled around like a model on a runway. "Pretty classy, huh? It's a publicity stunt to advertise the opening of the play. I'm going to do an announcement on the PA system this morning followed by personal appearances in all the homerooms. I look like a real Hollywood director, don't I?"

The initial shock of Jason's outlandish getup was starting to wear off. Holly stumbled forward. She was breathing hard from running across town. She grabbed onto Jason's lapels. "Where's Tisha?"

"Hey, watch the shirt!" Jason brushed her hands

away. He smoothed out the wrinkles. "I borrowed this from my uncle Travis and he'll be madder than a wet hen if—"

"Where's Tisha?"

Jason shrugged and looked around the empty classroom. "Not here," he said. "She never gets here this early. Nobody does. I only came early so I could get ready for my big promotional gig. You're ready, aren't you? I mean for the opening performance?"

Holly groaned. She'd forgotten *Dracula Meets the Los Gatos Panther* was set to open tonight. Too jittery to stand still, too upset to even bother to try to answer, she paced up and down the classroom aisles.

"You don't look ready." Jason shimmied his sunglasses down his nose and looked at her over the rims. "You look like you just rolled out of bed. Tut, tut, my dear," he said, slipping back into his very phony, not quite British accent. "Can't have our star looking pale and wan. You simply must get your rest before the curtain goes up tonight."

"No. What I simply must do is find Tisha." Holly wasn't more than two feet away from Jason, but she was screaming. She couldn't help herself.

Jason scratched one finger under his nose. "You upset about something?"

"Brilliant, Sherlock!" Holly snorted. She shook her head in disgust. From the blank expression on Jason's face, she knew he didn't have even the vaguest idea why she was so uptight. Still, she couldn't help but feel impatient. "Look," she said, "I've been all over town this morning. I can't find Tisha. Not

anywhere. She isn't at home. She isn't at her grandmother's store. So far, she's not here at school.''

Jason pulled off his sunglasses and tossed them and
his hat onto the nearest desk. Holly might be babbling
like a fool, but Jason didn't care. Already, his blue
eyes were dark as a lake on an autumn afternoon. He
was worried. Maybe not about Tisha, but about Holly.

He perched on the edge of a desk. "What happened?" he asked.

Holly threw her hands in the air. "I . . . I can't explain," she said. "I don't know where to start."

"How about at the beginning?" Hesitantly, Jason
put a hand on Holly's sleeve.

There was something about his touch that helped
quiet the fear that had been raging through Holly all
morning. She took a deep breath. She closed her eyes.

"All right," she said, her words tight and painful
in her throat. "The beginning. We were at the museum last night. Me and Tisha. We were down in the
temple when we heard it. The panther."

Holly opened one eye to see if Jason was laughing
yet. He wasn't. He looked serious. Like he did when
he talked about his dad's drinking problem.

Holly let go of the breath she'd been holding. "I
know it sounds crazy. But—"

"No. It's not crazy." Jason put a hand on Holly's
other arm. He looked her right in the eyes. He didn't
believe her. Not completely. She could tell it from the
look on his face. But that wasn't what mattered now.
What mattered was that he was listening. That he
cared.

"You know I don't believe in the panther," Jason said. "It's just a crazy story. But . . . well, whatever happened has got you all worked up. If it's enough to upset you, then it isn't crazy. It's serious. Real serious. Serious enough to make you all twitchy." He ran his hands up and down her arms. "You're quivering like a leaf in a windstorm. I'll tell you what, Holly." He got up and made a move toward the door. "Let's give your dad a call at the museum. If there was some kind of funny business there last night, he's bound to know about it."

"No." Holly shook her head. "You don't understand. You don't know the whole story yet. We were at the museum. And we heard the panther. But then . . . then all the lights went out. After that . . . after that, I don't know what happened." Holly couldn't possibly explain how she woke up in her own bed without knowing how she got there. How could she explain when she didn't understand it herself?

She decided on a compromise. Maybe half the truth would help more than none at all. "When the lights went back on, I couldn't find Tisha," she told him. "And this morning . . ." Holly sobbed, ". . . this morning I heard my dad talking on the phone to somebody real important-sounding. It must have been the police. They found a body at the museum, Jason. Oh, Jason!" Holly grabbed Jason and held on for dear life. "What if it's Tisha?" she asked, her voice breaking. "What can we do?"

Jason pulled her tight against him. He didn't mean anything by the hug. Holly knew that. It wasn't like when Alex held her close and telegraphed a thousand years' longing to every inch of her body.

It was nothing like that.

When Alex held her, she was sure she'd go up in flames. And when she did, no one had to tell her the fire would destroy them both. Somehow she knew that wasn't what Jason was looking for. Jason just wanted to show her he was there for her.

"Shh. It's okay." Jason stroked her hair. "How 'bout if we go check it out? Right now. We'll go down to the police station and see what we can find out. So what if we miss a few classes this morning?" Wrapping one arm around Holly's shoulders, Jason led her to the door.

"This is more important," he said. He gave one last, wistful look to his discarded hat and sunglasses. "Besides," he said, "I have the rest of my life to be a famous director."

The police wouldn't tell them a thing.

Holly wasn't surprised. Everyone was tiptoeing around the station like the place was made of eggshells. The officer at the desk turned beet red when they asked to see someone about the incident at the museum last night. He had them speak to the sergeant. The sergeant told them she didn't have the slightest idea what they were talking about. She told them to see one of the detectives. The detective assured them they had heard nothing more than a rumor. He sent them on to the chief.

The chief wouldn't see them. He was in a meeting; he would be all day.

Holly wasn't sure which was worse, the terrible gnawing feeling of worry in her gut, or the fact that everyone was treating them like they were making the whole thing up. She leaned back against the wall across from the conference room where the meeting was taking place, waiting for the opportunity to speak to the chief.

Nobody came out of the room, but once, when one of the officers came back from the local McDonald's with bags of food and trays of drinks, she did get a look inside. She could see there were a lot of people sitting around a long conference table. Her dad was one of them.

Holly tensed and made a move toward the open door. Too late. The door snapped shut again, but not before Holly's dad looked up and saw her. He immediately looked away, pretending she wasn't there.

"Let's get out of here." Jason sounded disgusted. Holly couldn't blame him. She'd had enough, too. There was no way they were going to find out anything here.

The rest of the day was one big blur.

After school, Holly went home long enough to grab a quick shower and change her clothes. Her mom was home; her dad wasn't. And still no one was saying anything about the body in the museum. She tried to call Tisha again and got no answer. She called the store. No answer there, either.

By the time Holly got back to school for the opening performance of *Dracula Meets the Los Gatos Panther*, she felt like she'd been in a food processor all day. Her head was spinning; her stomach was in knots.

She'd decided this morning that she wouldn't appear in the play at all. She'd let Tracy Powell, her understudy, do the part.

Thank goodness, Jason hadn't given her any of that "show must go on" nonsense. If he had, Holly was sure she'd have lost it. But that wasn't Jason's style.

He'd only explained, quietly and calmly, that she wouldn't accomplish anything sitting at home waiting for the phone to ring. The best place for Holly to be right now was with her friends, he told her. And they were all at school. He didn't admit that he wanted her there so he could keep an eye on her, but Holly knew it was true. It was so sweet, she couldn't say no.

Holly slipped into the auditorium and headed backstage. She had to fight her way through the crowd of crew members making last-minute adjustments to sets, carrying costumes, and getting programs ready to pass out at the door.

Jason was already on stage. She looked up long enough to see him. He was busy with some last-minute crisis, but he took the time to give her a reassuring wink when she went by.

One of the freshmen homerooms had been turned into the girls' dressing room. Holly dragged herself inside and slumped down in one of the chairs that was set in front of a bank of mirrors.

"You're the star of this thing. You're not supposed

to look all limp and wilty like yesterday's salad.''

Holly's head snapped up. Behind her in the mirror, she saw someone carrying a load of costumes so large, only the person's nose stuck out over the bundle. It was all Holly needed to see.

"Tisha!" Holly bolted out of her chair. She ran over to Tisha and grabbed her. "Tisha! You're here! You're really, really here!" Holly bounced up and down. She gave Tisha a bear hug that left Tisha squealing, and rumpled every last costume she was holding.

"You're here! You're here!"

"Of course I'm here." Tisha peered at Holly over the stack of costumes. She looked the way Holly supposed people looked when they weren't sure if you were crazy or not. "I'm supposed to be here. Remember? I'm in charge of costumes. I—"

"But you weren't here." By this time, Holly sounded like a tape recorder on fast forward. She knew she wasn't making any sense. She didn't care. Not even a little. "Not at your house. Not at the store. Not at school. Tisha! You weren't anywhere!"

"Well, of course I was." There was a clothes rack nearby and Tisha hung up the costumes she was carrying. "I was picking up my aunt Amy at the airport. Remember? She's the one who lives in Baltimore. She bought one of those last-minute fares and she couldn't fly into Portland, so we had to drive up to Seattle for her. We left at the crack of dawn. Holly, I told you all this stuff a couple weeks ago." Tisha made a face. "You don't remember anything anymore."

"The airport! The airport!" Holly felt like a fool. She was crying. She was laughing. She was jumping around. She was happier than she'd been in a long, long time. None of the other stuff mattered. Not right now. Not Laila's awful prediction or Alex's hurt feelings. Not the fact that Holly hadn't been able to find the amulet, or the mystery of how she'd gotten home from the museum last night.

All that mattered was that Tisha was here. That she was all right.

By now, Tisha wasn't the only one who was looking at Holly like she was nuts. Nearly the entire female cast and crew were here and they were all staring at her.

"She was at the airport!" Holly sniffed back her tears and, grabbing onto Tisha's shoulder, she beamed at the sea of stunned faces watching her. "Tisha was at the airport!"

Tisha gave the crowd a wobbly smile. She twined her arm through Holly's. "She's fine," she told everyone. "Holly's fine. Just a case of stage fright. She'll be as good as new as soon as she relaxes a little." With that, Tisha tugged Holly into the farthest corner of the room and forced her into a chair.

"Would you mind telling me what this is all about?" Tisha stood smack-dab in front of the chair so Holly couldn't pop out of it and start dancing around the room again.

For a second, Holly wondered if she really was crazy. After all that had happened at the museum last night, how could Tisha not be worried, too? Or maybe they never *were* in the museum last night? Maybe it was all a dream? "I was worried about you," Holly admitted.

Tisha scrunched up her nose. "You were?" she asked. "Why would you be? You're the one who left me that note."

"Note?" Holly looked at her in wonder. "I left you a note? What note?"

Now Tisha really did think she was nuts. Holly was sure of it. She tilted her head and looked at Holly suspiciously. "The note," she said. "The one signed Holly Callison? The one in your handwriting? I have to admit, if I didn't have the note, I would have been worried about you, too. I mean, after what happened in the museum last night."

Holly grabbed Tisha's hand. She would worry about the note later. She hadn't written it, but she thought she knew who did. "Then it wasn't a dream?" she asked Tisha. "We really were in the museum? We were there, and we heard the panther, and then all the lights went out. Am I nuts, Tisha, or did all that stuff really happen?"

"If you're nuts, then I am, too." Tisha went over to the costume rack and got the gown Holly was sup-posed to wear in the first act. It was a pretty dress, long and white. It had a square-cut neckline and lace all around the cuffs. "I have to admit, when the lights went off in that temple last night, I thought we were all goners." She motioned Holly to get up and waited while Holly stripped off her jeans and sweater. She slipped the dress over Holly's head.

Whoever made the costume did a great job. It was perfect down to the last detail, including the long row of buttons at the back. Tisha nudged Holly to turn around so she could start working on the buttons.

"But then the lights went on again." Tisha paused long enough to snap her fingers. "Just like that. But I wasn't in the museum anymore! I don't get it. I don't know how you did it. But there I was, on my own front porch! And that note you wrote me was in my hands. You know, the one where you told me not to worry. That the whole thing was a joke."

Tisha finished the last button and spun Holly around so she could check and see if the dress was all right. She didn't meet Holly's eyes.

"Seems kind of like a mean trick," she said. She adjusted the flounce of lace along the hem of the dress. "I mean, Joe's an old guy and—"

"Joe!" Holly felt all the happiness drain right out of her. "I was so worried about you, I forgot about Joe."

Tisha wasn't listening. There was a loose pearl bead on Holly's sleeve and Tisha went over to the dressing table, got her needle and thread, and worked on tightening it.

"But the police officer said the guard reported the body." Trying to make sense of the whole thing, Holly mumbled to herself, "I figured it had to be you, because Joe was the one who called it in this morning."

"I don't know what you're talking about," Tisha said, snapping off the thread with her teeth. "And I don't know what Joe called in to who, but it sure wasn't this morning. Joe's the night guard, remember? There's a different guard at the museum in the morning."

Tisha was right.

The news sunk into Holly slowly, like a lead weight drifting to the farthest depths of a very deep well. It hit bottom with a sickening jolt, and Holly knew the truth.

Of course it wasn't Tisha's body at the museum. Tisha was alive and well.

It was Joe's.

Joe Pendergrast was the one who'd been killed.

15

"Ah, fair Camilla."

Dracula bowed low over Camilla's hand and kissed the tips of her fingers.

Holly shivered. It was okay for her to tremble when Alex touched her, she told herself. Camilla was supposed to get all jelly-kneed when she met Dracula. What Holly hoped was that no one in the audience could tell that she wasn't acting.

Holly slapped away the thought.

Dracula—Alex, she corrected herself—didn't show any signs that the kiss had meant anything at all to him. It was what he was supposed to do in the play. That's all. And he did it with dramatic flair, swirling his black cape around him when he stood up, gliding over to the other side of the stage where, according to the script, he was supposed to meet the rest of the cast of characters.

Holly took a deep breath and used the time to try to compose herself. After the introductions, Dracula had to give a long, impassioned speech about the beauty of the night. It would take a couple minutes, Holly knew. By then she'd better get a grip on herself.

Holly moved into place in back of the red plush sofa that was set on one side of the stage. Camilla was supposed to be fascinated with the mysterious Count Dracula. She was supposed to be intrigued. She wasn't supposed to take her eyes off him.

That wouldn't be tough.

Holly had the feeling that even if the script called for Camilla to ignore Dracula completely, she wouldn't be able to tear her eyes away from Alex tonight.

He looked fabulous in the black tuxedo the costume crew had rented for him. It had been a couple weeks since Holly had paid much attention to Alex—since the day of their awful fight over Jason's Valentine's message. Holly hadn't noticed that he was letting his hair grow. He wore it pulled back from his face and tied at the base of his neck in a thick ponytail.

Most guys would look awful with their hair so tight against their heads, Holly decided. Alex looked incredible. His green eyes flashed in the bright stage lights. His hair sparkled with blue-black highlights.

He was every inch mysterious.

Every inch Dracula.

The thought unnerved Holly and, for a second, she lost track of where she was and what she was doing there.

"My daughter, Camilla, will accompany you into dinner, Count Dracula."

Holly snapped out of it just in time to catch the line spoken by Ben, who played her father in the play. It was her cue to do something.

If only she could remember what.

Running her tongue over her lips, Holly looked at

Ben. She looked at Alex. She looked at Jason who was standing in the wings. He had a copy of the script in his hands and he should have been able to prompt her. He would have, if he wasn't standing there with his eyes shut tight and a sour expression on his face, like he was the one who was out on stage forgetting his lines and making a spectacle of himself.

Alex came to the rescue. He swept across the stage to Holly's side. Even though she was sure it wasn't in the script, he took her hand.

"I shall be more than happy to spend the evening with this lovely creature," he said to Ben. He turned and looked into Holly's eyes. "We are destined for each other, Camilla and I," he said, and he lowered his voice to a whisper meant only for Holly's ears. "We have been, for all time."

"If you keep forgetting your lines, you're going to screw up this whole play."

Alex gave Holly a stinging look. He downed the last of a Coke and tossed the empty can to a crew member who was standing close by, waiting to raise the curtain.

Holly ignored the look, just like she ignored the fact that everyone around them seemed to be watching. Word about Holly and Alex breaking up traveled around the school with the speed of light. By now, everybody knew they hadn't spoken in weeks. The fact that they were talking now must have qualified as the juiciest sort of gossip possible.

"I've been a little preoccupied." Holly kept her

voice down so that no one could hear it, not even the kid working the curtain. "I can't seem to forget our little adventure in the museum last night."

Alex snorted. He straightened his bow tie. "I don't know what you're talking about," he said.

"Don't you?" Holly raised her chin and looked him in the eye. "I suppose you're going to tell me you don't know anything about Joe either? Joe Pendergrast? I'm not stupid, Alex. I don't need to wait to see it in the paper. I know that was Joe's body they found this morning. I think you know what happened. And I think you owe me an explanation."

She never knew if Alex was going to give her one.

The curtain went up and Alex swung her into his arms. This was the big ballroom scene, and they were supposed to waltz onto the stage together.

The music was provided by four members of the wind ensemble who had volunteered their services for the evening. They were pretty good. The melody was pretty. The beat was spellbinding.

"*Joe was dangerous.*" Alex sent the message into Holly's head. She should have blocked it out, just like she'd blocked out all his other attempts to communicate with her these last couple weeks. But she was too busy trying not to trip over her own feet, too busy making sure she didn't bump into the other cast members who were swirling around the ballroom, too busy praying that this time she would remember her lines. She didn't have the skill to raise her mind shields and do all that other stuff, too.

"*He knew things he shouldn't have known, Holly.*

He knew about you. He was dangerous."

"*Are you admitting it?*" Holly asked. She was still swaying to the music, but her mind reeled at the thought. It wasn't possible, was it? It wasn't possible that Alex . . .

Holly swallowed the sour taste in her mouth.

"*Are you admitting you had something to do with Joe's death?*" she asked, even though she was pretty sure she didn't want to hear Alex's answer. "*Are you admitting that you . . . you hurt Joe? Please, Alex.*" Tears sprang to her eyes. "*Tell me it isn't true. Please! I can't believe that. Not of you.*"

Alex's eyes lit with a smile. "*Of course I didn't hurt the old guy. Not intentionally.*" He swung her around the bulky dining room table that was set in the center of the stage. "*You know I wouldn't do that.*"

Alex's voice purred in Holly's head. The lights whirled around her. The music played on and on, until the whole world seemed filled with it. Lights and music. Alex's voice, and Alex's touch, and Alex's eyes staring down into hers. Pretty soon Holly couldn't feel her feet touching the floor anymore. She couldn't tell where the stage stopped and the audience began. All she could feel was Alex's arms around her and the terrifying, intimate brush of his mind against hers.

"*I wanted to scare Joe. That was all.*" Alex whirled her across the stage again. Something told Holly the music should have stopped a long time ago. But it didn't. It kept playing.

"*I wanted to scare him so he'd stop sticking his*

nose where it didn't belong. I never meant to hurt him.''

''*But you did.''* A tear rolled down Holly's cheek. She didn't have a chance to brush it away. ''*You scared him so bad, he . . .''* The sound of the music covered her sob. ''*. . . he had a heart attack or something, didn't he?''*

Alex didn't have a chance to answer. All of a sudden, the music ended, like someone hit the STOP button on a CD player in the middle of a song.

The actors froze in place and eyed one another. In the wings, Jason slapped his forehead with the palm on his hand.

Holly looked around.

She knew they were all waiting for her.

She cleared her throat.

''Dearest Drac.'' Holly grabbed both of Alex's hands and looked into his eyes. She wasn't supposed to say these lines yet. Not until the next act. She knew that even as they started to tumble out of her mouth— but she couldn't help it. ''Don't you know how I long to be with you?''

''*Do you long to be with me*?'' Alex's voice rang in her head.

''When you are out . . . when you are out in the dark . . .''

''*I asked you a question, Holly*!'' Alex smiled down at her. With one finger, he traced the line of her jaw, all the way from her ear to her chin.

It was bad enough having Alex's voice in her head—the feel of his hand against her skin was too much to take. Holly wanted to close her eyes. But she couldn't. She wanted to look away. But that was impossible. She kept her gaze fixed on Alex. On his eyes. On his face. On his lips. And she couldn't keep his voice out of her head.

"Do you long to be with me, Holly? Do you think about me as much as I think about you? I was angry with you, I admit it. But I realize now that it wasn't your fault. You can't help what Jason does. You're so beautiful, he can't help but love you. I'll forgive you, Holly. But you have to tell me, do you want to be with me? Forever and ever?"

"*Not now, Alex,*" Holly pleaded. Even inside her own head, her voice sounded shaky and on the edge of tears. "*Don't try to talk to me now. I've got to concentrate on my lines. You're getting me all mixed up.*"

"*It has to be now!*" Alex didn't seem to care that they were on stage in front of a couple hundred people. A couple hundred people who were waiting for the play to continue. Holly could hear them shifting in their seats, whispering to each other. "*Are you telling me the truth this time, Holly? Do you really mean it when you say you want to be with me?*"

Holly's brain froze. Her stomach turned into a block of ice. Suddenly she felt like she had the night of the deer hunt—like she was watching the world from inside a glass bubble. There was no one outside. Nobody left. And on the inside . . . on the inside there was only her . . . and Alex.

"*Say it, Holly!*" Though Alex looked as pleasant

as ever, his words sounded angry. They hurt inside her head. They settled in her heart. They seized her soul.

"Tell me the last few weeks have all been a mistake, Holly. Say you still love me."

"But you lied! About the blood. You didn't tell me that when we're adults—"

Holly didn't even realize she was talking out loud until she saw Jason in the wings. His face was pale and he was waving at her like crazy. "What are you talking about?" He mouthed the words.

Holly flinched and looked around. She'd forgotten where she was. Her voice shook with embarrassment. She stumbled her way back into her lines. "When . . . when you're out . . . out in the dark hunting your prey, can't you feel me there at your side, eager to take part in the feast?"

"The feast! Oh, Holly!" Alex's chest rose and fell. He scooped Holly into his arms.

Now Jason knew for sure that something was wrong. He was jumping up and down, pointing to his script and shaking his head.

But Holly couldn't have moved if she wanted to. Alex's arms were tight around her. His eyes were locked with hers, holding her with their power.

"It was all a mistake." This time his words were a gentle whisper in her mind. *"I know it was. You realize that now, don't you? I can feel your heart tell me. You know you were wrong. You know you can't deny your heritage. You can't deny fate. You are one with me, Holly. One with the goddess."*

"One with you. One with the goddess."

Holly whispered the words against Alex's lips, her gaze still fixed on his.

"That's it." Alex didn't even try to speak to her mind. He didn't need to. Not anymore. He knew she was his.

Body and soul.

Alex's face split with a smile as smooth as a knife blade.

With a swirl of his cape, he loosened his hold on Holly and crossed the stage. Over in the far right corner was a table. On it was the cup Dracula was supposed to give Camilla to drink later in this act. Jason had insisted that they use a glass mug so everyone in the audience could get the full effect of the cherry Kool-Aid they were using to look like blood.

Alex lifted the mug to the light. The red liquid inside gleamed.

He took a long drink. And he smiled.

Crossing the stage, he offered the cup to Holly.

"This isn't where this is supposed to happen!" Jason wasn't even bothering to mouth the words anymore. He was speaking in a stage whisper, a loud stage whisper, and jumping up and down like his feet were on fire. Tisha was standing next to him, a costume slung over her shoulder. She was tearing through his script, trying to find the right page so she could help them get back on track.

Holly barely noticed. She took the cup from Alex because she couldn't do anything else. She had to do whatever he wanted. She stared down into the crimson liquid for what seemed like an eternity. It was dark and red and heavier-looking than any Kool-Aid she'd ever seen. She raised the cup to her lips.

Suddenly everything started to spin.

Like it was the only thing that could keep her from falling, Holly held onto the cup with both hands. Trying to steady herself, she took a deep breath.

Her stomach jumped into her throat.

And that's when she knew.

She knew it as sure as she was standing there.

The cup was full of Joe Pendergrast's blood.

How long she stood there paralyzed with horror, Holly didn't know. Like the memory of a dream, she heard someone call her name.

"Holly! Holly!"

It wasn't Alex. He was standing right in front of her, and Holly didn't have to see him to know that he was smiling.

It wasn't any of the other cast members. She could feel their eyes on her. They were shifting self-consciously from foot to foot. They were clearing their throats. They were glancing at one another as casually as they could and wondering what in the world was going on.

It wasn't Tisha. Tisha was too busy staring with her mouth wide open.

"Holly!"

Holly yanked her gaze away from the gruesome liquid. She looked into the wings, over to where Jason stood calling her name. He wasn't jumping up and down anymore. He was just standing there, his hands at his sides, both palms turned out to her like he was there to catch her if she fell. His blue eyes were dark with worry. His cheeks were red, and Holly knew he wasn't embarrassed because she forgot her lines or because his play was ruined. He was angry. He was afraid. He was filled with some strong emotion Holly couldn't even begin to understand.

She looked from Jason to the cup in her hands, and from the cup to Alex.

She was right.

Alex was smiling. His lips were still wet with blood.

"*You had me worried.*" With one graceful movement, Alex poised his finger under the cup and lifted it toward Holly's lips. His voice was warm and satisfied. "*I doubted your loyalty. I questioned your devotion to the goddess. Prove that I was wrong. Show me I can still trust you.*"

The blood smelled delicious, far more appealing than the deer's blood had smelled the night of the hunt.

Holly's canine teeth tingled. She hoped no one noticed, but she could have sworn they grew a fraction of an inch. They felt longer. Pointier. She licked her lips.

"Drink and seal the bond between us." Alex raised his voice. What he was saying sounded so much like the lines of the play that no one in the audience suspected that anything was wrong. Now that things were moving again, they settled back into their seats and they were anxiously waiting to see what would happen to Camilla. In fact, a few of them really entered into the spirit of the play. Holly heard someone yell, ''Come on, Camilla! Drink the blood!'' from the back of the auditorium.

If she didn't know better, she could have sworn it was Laila.

''The blood of life!'' Alex's voice soared up to the open rafters above the stage and echoed back at her. ''The blood of death! Drink, Camilla, and show the world you love me!'' He nudged the cup up to Holly's lips.

''Holly!'' Jason ran on stage and Holly saw Alex's eyes flash with anger.

Either Jason didn't notice, or he didn't care. He skidded to a stop.

''Don't do it, Holly!''

''You mean Camilla!'' someone called out. There was a burst of applause and a lot of laughter as the audience joined in what they thought was all part of the show.

''Holly, I don't know what's going on, but I know you don't want to do this.'' Jason took a step forward, slowly, like he was approaching a wild animal.

''I . . .'' Holly blinked into the bright light. ''I want . . . I don't want . . .'' She looked from Alex to Jason. She looked down into the cup.

By now her hands were shaking so bad that the blood sloshed over the sides of the cup. It was warm and sticky on her fingers.

Like it was all happening in slow motion, Holly

watched the blood splatter against her white dress. She stared at the bizarre patterns it made as it drizzled to the floor.

From the corner of her eye, she saw Jason make a move toward her. She saw Alex with his teeth bared, his mouth open in rage. His shoulders were up, like the hackles of an angry animal.

She saw the blood. And she knew that no matter what Alex said, Joe didn't die of a heart attack. He didn't die by accident. If he did, she wouldn't be standing here with his blood all over her hands.

Holly lifted her fingers from the cup. One at a time.

The glass mug slipped out of her hands. It dropped to the floor and sat there, sparkling in the stage lights like a clear, shiny boat in a lake of blood.

With a scream wrenched from her soul, Holly ran off the stage.

16

Holly was sure no one would find her in the library. It was up on the third floor of the school and the auditorium was on the first floor. It was the last place anyone would bother to look for her.

She didn't know how long she planned to hide up here. Sooner or later, she'd have to come down.

It might as well be later, she decided.

It was bad enough that eventually she'd have to see Jason and face the music for ruining his play. But she knew that sooner or later, she'd have to see Alex, too, and she wasn't sure what she would do then.

Holly shivered. She wrapped her arms around herself, but that didn't help. Not even a little. No matter how hard she tried, she couldn't stop. She was shaking from head to toe. She was crying. Her throat hurt from screaming. Her head pounded and her eyes burned and there was a pain so far down deep inside her, she wished she could fall to the floor and never, ever get up again.

She prayed that the darkness would swallow her, that it would close up around her and never let her out again. She wanted to be alone. Completely alone. Forever and ever and ever.

She should have known better.

The library doors swung open. The thought that someone had come looking for her only made Holly feel worse. She pressed her hands to her mouth to stifle her sobs, and hoped that whoever it was wouldn't find her in the dark.

She felt even worse when she saw who it was.

Jason came into the library and stopped just inside the doors, looking around. He was out of breath from running up the steps. Even though the library was lit only by the red exit signs above the doors, Holly could tell his face was flushed with excitement. His eyes lit when he saw the glow of her white dress in the dark. He hurried over to her.

"I don't know what that was all about, but the audience loved it. Can you hear them? They're still clapping!"

Jason was smiling like a loon. He brushed one hand through his hair. "I wish you guys would have told me you had that planned. You had me worried for a minute. First I thought you just forgot all your lines. Then I thought maybe something funny was going on. Something weird." He jiggled his shoulders to get rid of the feeling. "Then I realized you and Alex must have had it planned all along. What a great bit! Especially the stuff about the blood of life and the blood of death. I wish I'd written that! Why didn't you tell me you were going to do that? Huh, Holly? Holly?"

It didn't take long for Jason to realize Holly wasn't nearly as happy about the play as he was. He bent down and gave her a closer look and all the excitement drained out of his face. "Holly?" He grabbed her shoulders. "Are you okay?"

If Holly thought she was miserable before, she was wrong. Nothing could make her feel worse than the thought that Jason cared about her. She burst into tears.

Jason pulled her into his arms. He ran his hands up and down Holly's back, trying to calm her. The enthusiasm was gone from his voice. It was quiet now. Thoughtful. And suddenly edged with something very close to fear. "I've been a real jughead, haven't I?" Jason asked. "None of that stuff was planned. Something happened out there and I was too stupid to stop it." He held her at arm's length. "I'm sorry. I should have—"

"No." Holly shook her head. "You couldn't stop it then. You can't stop it now. No one can. Not ever. Jason, I—"

No matter how hard she tried, Holly couldn't say any more. She wrapped her arms around Jason, buried her face in his chest, and cried until she didn't have any tears left. When she finally stopped, it was as if the world had melted away. All she could hear was the slow, steady beat of Jason's heart. All she could feel was the heat of his body, so close to hers, and the warmth of his arms around her.

"You don't have to go back down there," Jason finally said, his voice close to her ear. "Tracy will do the rest of the play. You can go home and relax, and by tomorrow you'll be yourself again."

"No!" For just a minute, Holly had felt so safe, she actually had convinced herself that the rest of the world didn't exist. Now, it all came rushing back at her. She pushed away from Jason. She threw her words at him, not because she was mad at Jason, but because she was mad at herself. Mad at the world.

"I won't be myself tomorrow," Holly screamed. "I'll never be myself again. I can't be. No matter how hard I try, I can't be Holly Callison anymore. She's gone. She's gone, Jason!" Holly was crying again. When Jason reached for her, she tried to fight him off, but she didn't have the strength.

Not when his hands were so gentle.

Not when there was so much tenderness in his eyes.

Holly's words dissolved into tears. "I can't be Holly anymore."

She heard Jason draw in a breath. He wrapped one arm around her shoulders and stroked her hair with his other hand. "Well, then, there's only one solution." He sounded so sure and confident. "I'll just have to love whoever it is you decide to be."

That did it.

Holly was crying full force now. Not because she was miserable anymore, but because Jason loved her.

She wondered how he could. She wondered if he would if he knew what she really was. And the thought nearly broke her heart.

When Jason kissed her, Holly didn't even try to resist. She couldn't. She let herself get lost in the warmth and the friendship and all the love he offered. She didn't think past the next minute, past the feel of Jason's lips on hers, or the feel of his hand where it pressed against her back.

Jason tightened his hold. "Holly." He breathed her name against her lips. "I never thought . . . I mean, I always wanted . . . I mean, I don't know what's going on with you and Alex. But I know you're not happy. I know you want out and I know you don't know how you're going to do it. Please don't worry anymore. I'll help. Anyway I can. I love you, Holly. I've been nuts about you from the minute I met you. You can't know how much this means to me."

"Oh, but I'm sure she can!"

Holly and Jason both jumped back, startled by the sound of Alex's voice.

Holly looked around the pitch-black library. There was no sign of Alex. He wasn't over by the doors. He wasn't near the card catalogue. He wasn't anywhere.

For a couple seconds, she figured she'd imagined the whole thing, but all she had to do was look at Jason to know she hadn't. Jason was looking around the room, too, his eyes wide. That's when Holly knew for sure. She'd heard Alex, all right. They'd both heard Alex. And though they couldn't see him, Holly was sure he was there.

Watching.

Too late, Holly remembered her dream.

She remembered how it all began last fall, with a dream about the school library.

And the panther that waited for her in the shadows.

Holly grabbed Jason's hand. "Let's get out of here," she said. She didn't wait for him to respond. She tugged him toward the door.

Just like in the dream.

The frightening thought rocketed through Holly's head and made every step between her and the door look like it was at least a mile long.

Just like in the dream, she groped her way through the darkness, terrified of the thing that prowled just beyond her field of vision. The thing that was watching her. The thing that was waiting for her.

The same thing that had haunted her every moment since the day she came to LGH and saw the panther on the wall.

Just like in the dream, Holly scrambled for the door. She didn't care how she got there, all that mattered was that she get out of the library as fast as she could.

But Jason wasn't part of the dream. Holly held on tight to Jason's hand, drawing courage from the thought.

In her dream, she was all alone. All alone, facing the panther.

But now she had Jason.

The thought lifted Holly's spirits and, for just a moment, she could have sworn some of the darkness in the library lifted, too.

The next thing she knew, Holly was out in the hallway.

Still holding onto Jason's hand, she sucked in a long breath.

"Could you take me home?" she asked. "Huh? Jason, could you?"

Jason wasn't listening. He was staring at the closed library doors. He shook his head. He tried his best to sound casual, but Holly knew he was nervous. She could smell it.

"You know," he said, "I could have sworn there was something in the library with us. Not Alex, even though I heard him. Well, I thought I heard him. This was something . . . something else." Jason rubbed one hand across his eyes as if that would help clear his head. He hauled in a ragged breath. "Maybe I'm just jittery from everything that happened this evening. I swear . . . I swear I saw something in there. Something black. It looked . . ." Jason's Adam's apple bobbed. "Holly, if I didn't know any better, I'd say it looked like a panther."

Holly didn't answer him.

There wasn't anything she could say.

She should have been relieved, she told herself, towing Jason down the stairs. Just like in the dream, she'd gotten out of the library safely.

But just like in the dream, she knew that the panther was still waiting for her. Somewhere outside.

> *Roses are red,*
> *Violets are blue.*
> *I know you've been avoiding me,*
> *But I really need to talk to you.*

Tonight? Panther Hollow? 8 o'clock. It's important.

Holly refolded the note from Jason and tucked it in her pocket. He was right, of course. She had been avoiding him.

She'd been avoiding everyone.

She'd convinced her mom and dad that she was sick. Sick enough to stay home from school these past few days.

She hadn't talked to a soul. Not since the night of the play.

But if she wanted to avoid Jason, what was she doing here in Panther Hollow waiting for him?

Holly stomped her feet against the cold and blew on her hands.

Because this wasn't like all the other notes Jason had sent her this week, she told herself.

It wasn't like the notes full of silly jokes and half-baked puns that asked why she didn't come to the phone when he called. Or even like the ones with frilly heart borders that asked if he could stop by and see her.

This note was short. And serious. Too serious.

Jason sounded worried. And after all he'd done for her, Holly couldn't stand the thought of that.

"Good of you to come!"

Holly swung around.

Though she hadn't heard him coming, Alex was there, not ten feet away. He was leaning against a tree, a sleek smile on his face.

All week, Holly had wondered what she'd say to him the next time they met. Now she was too surprised to even care. She stalked over to him. "What are you doing here?" she demanded.

"Roses are red. Violets are blue." Alex laughed. He straightened and stretched like a cat that had just gotten up from a nap, and pulled himself up to his full height.

Funny, in all the time they'd spent together Holly never realized how really tall he was.

She shook the thought aside and moved back a step. It was easier to see him from back here, she reasoned with herself. She didn't want to admit he didn't look nearly as threatening from farther away.

Alex was too busy looking pleased with himself to notice. "I know you've been avoiding me," he said in a singsong voice, "but I really need to talk to you." He smiled down at Holly. The light of a full moon glimmered in his eyes like the reflection of a fire off a knife blade. "It's important."

"That's a cheap trick!" Holly's temper shot up like a flare. "That note wasn't from Jason, was it? It was from you. Just like the note Tisha found the night Joe was killed at the museum."

Alex shrugged. It was an indifferent sort of movement, like the kind people make when they're pretending they're humble. "It's a nice little talent," he admitted. "The ability to fake other people's handwriting. It's fun to do every once in a while. And it comes in handy."

"Fun." Holly grumbled. She couldn't stand the self-satisfied smile on Alex's face a second longer. She spun around. "We have nothing to talk about," she said.

"But we do." Before she had a chance to figure out what was going on, Alex had her turned around again. His hand was on her arm, gripping it so hard it hurt. "We have lots to talk about," he said.

Before, his voice was as sweet as honey. Now it was cold. Cold as ice. "I gave you a chance, Holly," Alex said. "At the play. I gave you a chance to show your loyalty. You disappointed me. But you're a lucky girl. You'll have another chance. Tonight. One last chance for you to make up your mind."

Alex stepped back.

For a minute, Holly didn't know what he was doing, what he was waiting for. Then she heard it, out in the woods. The sounds of footsteps and voices.

No.

The awareness sunk into Holly like the bite of cold steel.

Not voices.

One voice.

Jason's voice.

"All right. You've had your fun. How 'bout if you take this thing off and tell me what's going on."

Jason stumbled into the Hollow. He was surrounded on all sides by the other shape-shifters. He was wearing a blindfold and his hands were tied in front of him. He didn't look upset. He just looked confused. Like he knew someone was playing a trick on him and he wasn't quite sure yet what the joke was all about.

Holly took a step forward, but Alex was still holding her. And he wasn't about to let her go. She shot him a look. "What the hell's going on here?" she asked.

"Holly?" Jason heard her voice and his face split with a grin. "Holly? Is that you? Tell these jokers to get this thing off, will you?"

With a nod, Alex signalled to Tom, who whipped off Jason's blindfold.

Jason stood there in the middle of the Hollow, blinking at them all like an owl that had been flushed out of the woods.

"So, what's going on?" Jason smiled over at Holly. He looked at Alex, then ran his gaze over Raymond, Amber, Lindsey, Tom, and Laila. "What's up, guys? What's this all about?"

"What is this all about?" Holly shook off Alex's hand. "If this is some kind of sick gimmick to try to get us back together again, Alex—"

"Oh, it's not a joke." Smooth as a snake, Alex glided over to Jason. With one quick flick of his fingers, he loosened the ropes from Jason's wrists.

"It's not a joke at all," he said. He dangled the ropes from one finger, his gaze sliding from Jason to Holly. "This is it. Your choice, Holly. Tell me right now. Who will it be? Me?" He tipped his head toward Jason. "Or him?"

Holly stared at him in wonder. She would have liked to think that he was kidding, but she knew he wasn't. There was nothing like teasing in Alex's eyes. Nothing but hatred, and a jealousy so deep and cold, it froze her heart.

She knew what Alex wanted her to say, and right now she didn't care if it was true or not. She had to get Jason out of here as fast as she could. She knew that, too. And she could think of only one way to do that.

At the same time she stepped toward Alex, Holly shot a quick, apologetic look at Jason. She wasn't sure he saw it, but at least it made her feel better.

Holly drew in a long breath. Raising herself on her tiptoes, she kissed Alex, long and hard. It wasn't something he was expecting, but she could tell it was something he enjoyed. Alex flattened one hand against the small of Holly's back and deepened the kiss.

By the time he was done, Holly's knees felt shaky and it was hard to catch her breath. She stepped away, fighting to control herself, and kept her eyes on Alex. She had to. Jason looked like he'd just been sucker-punched, and she couldn't stand to see that.

Alex smiled down at her, but it wasn't the warm kind of smile that made the corners of his eyes crinkle. It was a hard smile. A cold smile. "Good choice!" he said. "You've said all the right things. And you've certainly done all the right things." He tucked one finger under Holly's chin and lifted it up so that his face was only inches from hers. "Now let's see if you mean it."

"What?" Holly couldn't help herself. Something in the way Alex looked at her told her she'd been tricked. And she didn't like that at all. "What are you talking about?"

Alex didn't answer. He sauntered over to Jason. "You have a half hour," he said, matter-of-factly. "A half hour to get as far away from here as you can."

He looked down at his watch, then up at Jason again. "Your time starts . . . now! You'd better get going."

"Huh?" Jason looked over at Holly. "I don't get it," he said. "This is some kind of joke, right?"

Holly didn't answer right away. She couldn't.

There was a sour taste in her mouth and her throat was tight, like there was an invisible hand around it, squeezing off her air.

Something told her it was coming to this. All along, it was headed right here.

Why hadn't she see that before?

Why hadn't she known it weeks ago, when she dreamed about the panther that attacked Jason in the newspaper office?

"It's not a joke." Holly's voice was thick. She couldn't let either Jason or Alex see the tears in her eyes, so she looked away. "You have a half hour, Jason," she said. "Just get out of here while you can."

"Why should I?" Jason bobbed around on the balls of his feet like a fighter getting ready to go into the ring. His hands curled into fists. He tossed a look at the other shape-shifters, not paying attention to the girls, but watching the guys like he expected them to jump him. "What are we talking about?" he asked. "Some sort of sick game of hide and seek? You guys against me? Sorry, that's not enough to scare this boy."

"Then maybe this will." Alex's words ripped through the Hollow like an icy winter wind. He changed so fast, even Holly stepped back in surprise.

An enormous panther stood in front of Jason, its eyes flashing fire, its fangs slick and pointed.

"Holy—!" Jason's eyes popped open wide. He ran his tongue over his lips and his face got pale. But he didn't flinch, and he didn't run. He held his ground.

"Then it's true." Holly wasn't sure if Jason was talking to them or to himself. "All the stuff about the panther. And the legend. You guys are . . . Are you telling me—"

"I'm telling you you've got a half hour to get out of here." In the blink of an eye, Alex was Alex again. He smoothed his ink-black hair with one hand and casually flicked back the sleeve of his expensive cashmere sweater so he could take a look at his watch. "I take it back. Not a half hour. Twenty-seven minutes. And"—he smiled—"a panther can cover a lot of ground in twenty-seven minutes. And believe me, after we're done with you . . ." Alex's face was as pleasant as ever, but his voice crackled with hatred. ". . . there won't be enough left of you for anyone to find. Every inch of your flesh will be gone. Every one of your bones. There won't even be a blood stain on the ground."

"Right." Jason nodded. He might be brave, but he wasn't stupid. He took a step toward the woods. "I'm out of here," he said, gesturing with both hands flat, as if commanding a dog to stay. "But not without Holly."

He turned to Holly and spoke to her like there wasn't anyone else there, just the two of them, sharing the secrets of their hearts. "You can say what you want to Alex," he told her. "But I can see the truth in your eyes. There's no way you want to be a part of this, Holly. I know that. I know you. Come on." He held out his hand to her. "Let's get out of here."

In all her life, Holly never wanted anything as desperately as she wanted to take Jason's hand. He was all that was good. All that was honest. All that was right with the world.

But she knew he didn't stand a chance against the shape-shifters. Not without her help.

Holly hitched her hands behind her back. It was the only way she could keep herself from taking Jason's hand. "I'm staying," she said, and she hoped her voice didn't give away the fact that her heart was breaking. "I have to, Jason. I'm one of them."

"No. You can't be." He dropped his hand to his side and backed away. "If you're one of them . . . you wouldn't . . ." Jason took another step back. "You couldn't be . . . You—"

"Go!" Holly screamed at him. "Go! Go! Go!" she screamed again and again. When Jason still didn't move, she did the only thing she could think to do to get him going.

She changed into a panther and, letting out a deafening roar, she slashed the air with her claws.

Jason ran off into the woods.

"Time's up!" Alex got up from where he was sitting and stretched his arms over his head. "Everyone ready?" He looked at the other shape-shifters. Laila and Tom had already changed. They were pacing the edge of the woods, eager to get on with the hunt. It didn't take long for Lindsey, Amber, and Raymond to change, too.

Ever since Jason had run off into the woods, Alex had been acting as pleased as could be. He smiled over at Holly. "Are you ready?" he asked.

"I think so." Holly hoped she sounded more confident than she felt. She wasn't sure she was ready. She wasn't sure what she was going to do. It was hard trying to come up with a plan when she knew Alex could eavesdrop on her thoughts at any time.

But it was now or never. She knew that. She knew she had no choice.

Like she always did, Holly waited for Alex to change first before she slipped into her panther shape. Like always, he watched while she did, and his eyes glowed with the secret satisfaction that, until tonight, had always made her feel so special.

"*You've never hunted a person before.*" Alex slid into the shadows along the edges of the woods and waited for Holly to join him. "*You have a lot to learn. It's not like deer. That's easy. It's more fun with humans. They're a little more clever, though not much.*" He chuckled. "*Your Jason will try to outrun us. He'll try to outsmart us. But we know he can't.*" Alex pulled to a stop at the edge of a clearing and signalled for Holly to go on ahead.

"*Only, Holly . . .*" He stopped her before she got too far. "*Don't think I don't know what that was all about. Back there, when you kissed me. You were trying to get Boy Jason off the hook, weren't you? Well,*

*it won't work. Not that easily. You still have to do
penance. For thinking about Jason. For letting him
kiss you the night of the play. I should punish you
right here and now, but I won't. I love you too
much for that. Instead I'm going to prove how much
I love you. I'm going to give you a great honor.
When we catch Jason...''* Alex's chest rose and
fell, his teeth glinted in the moonlight. *''...when
we catch him, I'm going to let you be the one who
gets to eat his heart.''*

Holly didn't respond. How could she? She was
completely numb—body, heart, and soul. She stared
at Alex, and when he signalled her to run on ahead,
she took the opportunity to get as far away from him
as she could.

Holly pulled to a stop near a small creek and
sniffed the air. There was no sign of Jason anywhere.

For a minute, she had a wild vision, a fantasy in
which Jason really did get away from the pack. He
was halfway home by now, she told herself. He was
safe and sound and as far away from danger as he
could be.

But as quickly as she pictured it, Holly knew there
was no way it was true.

It would take hours for Jason to find his way off
Harper's Mountain in the dark. And Jason didn't have
hours.

If Jason was around—anywhere—the panthers
would find him. And when they did...

Holly forced the thought out of her head. She had
to, or she knew she'd lose her nerve.

Raising her head, Holly sniffed the air again. She wasn't checking for Jason this time. She was checking for the other panthers.

Amber and Lindsey weren't too far away. She could tell.

Before she could talk herself out of it, Holly darted deeper into the woods. She wished she could say she had a plan, but she knew what she was thinking was way too shaky to be called a plan.

It was a hope.

Nothing more.

But it was the only hope she had.

Holly found Amber and Lindsey not too far away. They were picking through a pile of leaves and twigs, their paws scattering scraps every which way. Holly closed her eyes and told herself to concentrate. Hard.

"You're very tired, Lindsey. You are too, Amber. So tired. So very tired." She tried to use the same, soothing voice she'd heard Alex use when he was trying to hypnotize someone to do what he wanted. *"It's late. And it's dark. And you're so tired."*

Amber's head snapped up. So did Lindsey's, and Holly could tell from the looks in their eyes that they knew exactly what Holly was trying to do. But just as Holly hoped, Amber and Lindsey were lazy. Too lazy to even try to fight powers that were more highly developed than theirs.

"A nice, long nap." Holly yawned. Amber and Lindsey yawned, too. *"A nice, long nap in the soft, soft leaves."*

Amber dropped to the ground first. It didn't take Lindsey long to follow.

"*Yes*!" Holly congratulated herself. She wished Jason was there to give her a high five. The thought sobered her. She cocked her head, listening for any sounds that would tell her the other panthers had found Jason.

Nothing.

Holly turned to head back up toward the Hollow. It was time to take care of Tom and Raymond.

Laila would be tougher.

Holly looked down to where Tom and Raymond lay sound asleep in a dense circle of raspberry bushes.

Laila wouldn't be hypnotized so easily, she reminded herself. And Laila was far more dangerous.

A cold shiver snaked its way down Holly's back.

She ignored it.

And ran off into the woods to find Laila.

The ruined camp building looked more unreal than ever in the light of the full moon.

Every shadow was sharp as a dagger. Every window looked more than ever like an eye hole, gaping at Holly, blind and menacing.

Pressing herself as flat as could be against the worn wooden shingles, Holly peered around the corner to the front of the building. Laila was perched at the edge of the clearing. She was looking around, but Holly knew Laila didn't see her. The building hid her from Laila's view. She knew Laila couldn't smell her, either. Holly had made sure she circled around the clearing and came out downwind from Laila.

Holly watched as Laila's ears pricked. Her eyes narrowed, and Holly knew Laila's keen eyesight and sharp sense of smell were picking up everything in the woods. Every leaf and bush. Every small animal that scurried in the undergrowth. If Jason was anywhere around, Holly knew Laila would find him, too.

The thought made Holly's blood run cold. It made her heart pound. It made her wish she could attack Laila, right here and now, and get the whole thing over with.

But she knew that would never work.

Laila's powers weren't nearly as developed as Holly's, but they were certainly better than those of the other shape-shifters Holly had left sleeping in the woods. Hypnotizing would never work with Laila. Neither would a face-to-face confrontation. What Laila lacked in power, she'd make up for in malice, and she'd been storing up her hate against Holly for a very long time.

Holly forced herself to sit back and wait for the right moment.

It didn't happen for a very long time.

Holly's head came up. She heard a twig snap in the woods. Then another. Panthers were silent hunters. A panther would never give away its position to an enemy with a careless step. Holly knew that.

So did Laila.

Laila's tongue flicked around the edges of her mouth. She got up, stretched, and crept over to the path that led back into the forest.

Holly was sure she'd never known how panic really felt. Not until now. She had to do something to stop Laila. And she had to do it fast.

Quick as lightning, a memory flashed through her mind.

The night of the homecoming bonfire.

The voice from the woods that called her name.

It wasn't Tisha who had called her. Holly found that out. And that meant it must have been Alex. Holly took a deep breath. If Alex could do it, she could, too.

Holly changed into her human shape and cupped her hands around her mouth.

"Laila!"

Her voice echoed through the stillness of the forest.

Laila looked around.

"Laila! In here!"

Holly held her breath. Even to her, the voice sounded like Alex's. She wasn't sure how she did it and, right now, she didn't care. She tried again.

"Here in the building! I need . . . I need your help."

It worked.

Laila swung around and ran up the steps, two at a time.

It wouldn't take her long to figure out she'd been fooled. Even Laila was smart enough to know an empty building when she saw one.

Holly sprinted up the steps. The first time she'd been here, there was an old car seat just inside the door. Since then, someone had dragged it outside.

Holly lifted the seat and wedged it into the doorway.

"What? What's that?" She heard Laila's voice echo in her head. Laila wasn't skilled enough to convey her emotions when she sent a mind message, but Holly could tell she was outraged. She saw Laila's eyes as she paced back and forth inside the doorway: They were red with fury.

"Who's there?" Laila came over to the window and looked out. Fortunately, there wasn't one big window in the building.

Holly thanked her lucky stars.

The windows were divided into small panes, each one framed in wood.

Laila stuck her muzzle as far out as she could. She growled. *"You double-crosser. I knew you were never really one of us. What are you doing?"* Holly heard Laila's footsteps pad against the wooden floor as she raced back to the doorway. *"You can't keep me in here."* Laila threw herself against the car seat.

Luckily, it held, but only because Holly was on the other side, pressing against it with all her might. That might work for a while, she told herself, but not for long.

Holly looked around. There were some broken cinder blocks not far away, and a big, square board that would seal the door completely.

She set the board in front of the door, propped the cinder blocks against it, and waited for Laila to test it again.

She did, and the board never moved.

"You can't do this to me. You can't, you—" Laila's

thoughts broke down into a jumble of curses.

Holly changed into her panther shape. As she scrambled down the steps, she saw Laila at one of the windows, growling with fury.

It didn't matter. She was locked up tight.

Holly headed back into the woods.

There was only one thing left to do.

One more panther to face.

17

By the time Holly found Alex, he was on to Jason's scent. His nose to the ground, he wound his way through a tangle of bushes, every inch of him tensed and ready for the attack.

Holly fell into step behind him.

"*I can't find Laila anywhere.*" Alex was angry. "*What's wrong with her? What's wrong with all of them? Can't they follow a simple trail?*"

"*It's okay.*" Holly reached out to him with her mind, stroking his ego, hoping to keep him off guard. "*I'm here. We don't need the others.*"

She heard Alex purr and congratulated herself. So far, he didn't suspect a thing.

Holly stood by Alex's side while he clawed his way through a tangle of vines. She watched as he broke into a run. She ran after him.

By now, she'd caught Jason's scent, too. It prickled along her skin. It caught at the back of her throat. It sizzled through her bloodstream, as clear and dazzling as the moonlight. Instinctively, she followed it, and it wasn't long until she saw Jason up ahead, fighting his way through an especially dense area of undergrowth.

Somehow, he sensed the panthers behind him. Jason whirled around.

The change in him was enough to make Holly cry.

Jason, who had always been so friendly.

Jason, who had always been so trusting.

Jason, who not more than a week ago had told her he loved her.

Jason was standing with his back to a tree. His expression was guarded and suspicious. His eyes were dark with terror. His face was pale. He had a heavy branch in one hand, a big, square rock in the other. When he saw them, he raised the stick, ready to defend himself.

In a flash, Alex changed into his human shape. Jason was immune to the switch by now. He barely batted an eyelash.

"There's no use fighting." As a human, Alex's face was much more animated. He couldn't even begin to hide his jealousy as he looked at Jason. "You don't stand a chance. Not against the two of us. We've already decided." He smiled over at Holly. "Holly gets your heart."

Jason looked over at Holly. His jaw was firm. His face was rigid. Only the thin ribbon of sweat on his upper lip betrayed how scared he was.

"Holly's always had my heart," Jason said. "But, Alex, I'll be damned if I let you get a piece of it." He raised the branch and charged.

The unexpected attack was enough to catch Alex off guard. At least for a second.

Holly saw her opportunity and took it.

Before he had the chance to change back into his

panther shape, she leapt and knocked Alex to the ground.

"What!" Alex's mouth fell open in surprise. He struggled beneath the weight of the panther, twisting around so that it was hard for Holly to get a hold of him. Only once, their eyes met. And Holly knew that Alex had figured out what was going on. He'd been betrayed. He knew it. And the realization filled him with hatred.

Still on top of Alex, Holly darted a look toward Jason.

"*Get out of here! Fast!*" She sent the message even though she wasn't sure Jason was at all capable of receiving it.

Maybe he was.

Maybe he wasn't.

Holly didn't have the chance to find out.

It only took an instant to try to communicate with Jason, but it was too long.

It was all Alex needed.

Holly felt Alex's muscles ripple beneath her. She felt the fur on his legs grate against hers. She felt the heat of his breath and sting of his teeth when they sank into her left foreleg.

Holly howled and backed off.

"*You dare?*" Alex jumped to his feet.

She'd seen him as a panther a hundred times before, but she'd never seen him like this.

His eyes flashed fire. His voice boomed in her head like thunder. "*You dare oppose me? You dare choose this human over me? You don't have a chance and you know it, Holly. I'll show you. You won't have to worry about eating this human's scrawny heart. You'll watch me do it. Right before I tear out yours!*"

His claws flashing, Alex jumped at her. He landed one blow to Holly's shoulder, another to her right front leg.

Holly reeled and fell on the ground. Her shoulder felt hot, like it was on fire, and she knew she was bleeding.

She rolled out of the way, just in time to see that Jason hadn't gone anywhere. Silently, Holly cursed him for his bullheadedness and his stupidity. She didn't have a chance to do more. Alex's claws slashed through the air, no more than an inch from her head. Struggling to her feet, Holly turned to face him, her fangs bared.

"*I always knew you had it in you.*" Alex circled around her. He was no less angry and he was certainly still jealous. Yet Holly couldn't help but think he would have been smiling if he could. "*You're a warrior. Just like me. We share our hunger for blood.*"

"*This has nothing to do with blood.*" Holly moved so that she was standing between Jason and Alex. "*It has everything to do with what's right and what's good. If you think I'm going to let you destroy Jason just because he kissed me, you'd better think again.*"

"*All for a kiss.*" Again, Alex's mocking tone howled through her head. "*I hope it was worth it.*"

With that, Alex came at her again. He was far larger than Holly and a much more skillful fighter. He saw every opening, and he used each to his best advantage.

He ripped into Holly's shoulder. His teeth tore into her neck. He knocked her to the ground again.

Holly dragged herself up. There wasn't much more she could do now. She knew that. Already she was feeling lightheaded from the loss of blood. She couldn't do anything more to hurt Alex, but she still might be able to help Jason.

"*Get out of here!*" She darted a look over her shoulder to where Jason stood watching the fight. He must have been in shock. His eyes were wide. His face was ashen. And he didn't look like he was about to move an inch.

"*Get out now!*" Holly tried again. To buy Jason some time, she lunged at Alex. She swiped her claws at him. This time, she met flesh, then bone, and Alex's blood streamed out and over her paw.

Her victory didn't last long. With incredible speed, Alex turned the tables on her. Before Holly knew what had happened or what was going on, she was pinned beneath Alex.

He glared down at her, his eyes blazing, his teeth wet with saliva and flecked with blood.

Holly's vision went out of focus. When it snapped back in again, she was looking at the cold, blue creature from the gazebo. She knew then what it was she'd seen that night.

"*You!*" She was out of breath, and it hurt her head to even try to communicate with Alex. But she kept on. She had to. She had to tell him she knew. "*It was you! You're the one who burned Jason's script. You. Your hatred. Your jealousy. You burned the gazebo.*

*You killed Joe and Mr. Tollifson. Not because they
knew too much. That's what you wanted me to think,
but it isn't true. You did it for pleasure. You did it
because you're filled with hate. You were lying to me,
weren't you, Alex? You were lying when you said you
loved me. There's no room in your heart for love."*

Alex never flinched. It was the only proof Holly
needed that everything she was saying was true. She
couldn't hurt him physically. Not anymore. She
couldn't hurt him with the truth. He didn't care. But
maybe she could still hurt his pride.

"Well, guess what?" Holly tried to sound cocky.
If she was in her human form, she knew she'd be
crying. *"I was lying, too. I may have loved your
beauty and your power. I may have been taken in by
all your charm. But I never loved you. Never."*

"Shut up!" Alex slammed one massive paw into
the side of Holly's head. *"Don't you ever say that.
Don't ever say you don't love me. It isn't true. I know
it isn't true. You love me, Holly. You have for all
time."*

Alex's voice faded in and out. Holly's vision
blurred and cleared and blurred again. The strange
blue phantom of hate was gone and all she could see
was Alex. His fur. His teeth. His eyes.

A strange euphoria filled Holly's head.

She was going to die. She knew that for sure now.
But at least when she did, she'd have the satisfaction
of dying with dignity. At least she'd die as a human
being.

With her last ounce of strength, Holly changed into her human form.

If she surprised Alex, he didn't show it. He bared his fangs and lowered his mouth to her throat.

Holly wasn't sure how it felt to die. She wondered how much it would hurt. She didn't know what she'd feel. She wasn't sure what she'd hear. Whatever it was, she was pretty sure it shouldn't have been the sickening thud that she did hear.

The next thing she knew, Alex's body was slumped over hers.

Holly looked up. Jason was standing over her. He had a rock in his hands, the same one he'd used to smash Alex on the head.

"Come on!" Jason grabbed Holly's hand and pulled her out from under the panther. He stooped down and helped her to her feet. "Let's get out of here."

"No." Holly shook her head. Her knees were wobbly, her shoulder and neck were still bleeding. She knew she'd never be able to move fast enough to get them off Harper's Mountain before Alex regained consciousness. "Just go on." She gave Jason a push. "You've got to get out!"

"Not without you." Jason didn't wait for her to argue anymore. He wrapped one arm around her shoulders and led her into the woods.

How long they stumbled through the dark, Holly didn't know. It seemed like years. But finally, they staggered out onto the road.

Holly slumped against Jason's shoulder. "You

shouldn't have saved me." She couldn't bear to look him in the eye. "Now you see what I am."

Holly must have been in shock. She could have sworn she heard Jason chuckling. She looked up to find him smiling down at her. "I know you're brave," he said. "You saved my life."

Jason brushed a long strand of Holly's hair out of her eyes. "I know you're beautiful," he said. "Even when you're covered with dirt." He rubbed a smear of dirt off her cheek. "I know now what's been bothering you since last fall. Why didn't you tell me? Why didn't you let me help? You were crazy to try to handle that alone. You see what they are!" He darted a look back to the woods. "You see the kind of people . . . the kind of creatures they are. I can't stand the thought of you taking all that on yourself. All alone."

Holly closed her eyes and leaned against Jason. After all these months . . . all the terrible dreams . . . all the worries . . . to share, finally, with someone.

Holly jerked to attention as a terrible roar echoed from the woods. There was no sign of Alex, but from the sound, he couldn't be far away.

"I think we'd better get out of here." Jason looked toward Panther Hollow. He didn't wait for Holly to say anything; he started off down the road, holding Holly's hand tight in his.

They walked in the middle of the road where they had a better chance of seeing Alex if he came out of the woods. How they missed him, Holly never knew.

One instant the road in front of them was empty.

The next, he was there. Back in his human form. Radiant in the moonlight.

Alex stood with his hands on his hips, his feet slightly apart. Every hair was in place. Every piece of his clothing looked like it had just come from the cleaners. If it wasn't for the long scratch on his right cheek, Holly would have wondered if she imagined the whole, terrible night.

"So, you've made your choice." Alex's voice was perfectly calm. "Is this what you want, Holly?"

Holly let go of Jason's hand and went to stand in front of Alex. She looked him in the eye. All she could think of was how being this close to him always used to make her feel. Light, like a butterfly. Weightless, like the bubbles in a glass of soda pop. Spirited, like a fireworks display.

Now, all she felt was disgust.

"Yes," she said. "I've made my choice. Life over death. My human form over the Gift."

Alex didn't move a muscle. His eyes were dark with pain. "I loved you," he said.

Holly refused to give in. Her shoulder ached. Her head hurt. Her heart was broken in a million pieces. Still, she held her ground. "I know." She didn't look away. "I'm sorry."

"Sorry?" Alex threw back his head and laughed. The sound of it was as cold as the night air. "You don't know anything about sorry. Not yet." He turned and stalked off down the road, and even after the darkness enveloped him, they could hear the chilling sound of his laugh reverberating through the night air.

And once, just once, they heard his voice. It echoed back at Holly and Jason like the deep, pulsing sound of a funeral bell.

"You'll be sorry all right, Holly," Alex said. "You've made your choice. From now on, we're at war!"

**Don't miss
WHISPERS FROM THE GRAVE**

The similarities between Jenna and Rita were un-
canny. They looked and acted exactly alike. Each
was experiencing the thrill of first love. Each was
enpowered with a gift of the supernatural. And
each harbored dark secrets. Jenna and Rita could
have been sisters. Except for one thing . . .

Rita was murdered over a century ago.

*Turn the page for a special sneak preview
of this exciting new suspense novel
by Leslie Rule!
Available now from Berkley Books*

Sometimes I wished I'd never found Rita's diary. If I'd known all the trouble it would cause, I would have left it in its hiding place. But how could I have known that little musty book with its yellowing pages and rusty keyhole would get me involved in a murder?

My neighbor, Suki, was with me when I found the diary. We were poking around the attic of my family's old, rambling house.

It was built way back in 1870 and was actually made from real wood. That's rare here on Puget Sound. The old blind man who lived across the street said they stopped using wood to build houses around 2035 because of the tree shortage.

Suki's house was made from fiberglass and never needed to be painted like our funky old house did.

"Ick! A spider!" Suki suddenly shrieked. It skittered across the dusty floor on its thick, feathery legs and disappeared into a crack in the attic wall.

"It won't hurt you," I said. "We're used to spiders here. This house isn't airtight like yours. There are lots of places for bugs to get in."

She shuddered, her shoulders rising so they touched the ends of her limp blond hair. "Let's go back downstairs to your room where there aren't as many bugs."

"Go ahead," I said and was relieved when she didn't. Last time she was alone in my room, I think she filched my new tube of strawberry lip tinter.

Suki had acted like my shadow ever since we moved to Banbury Bay in July when Mom inherited Great-aunt Ashley's old house. Just because Suki lived down the beach from us, and my father worked with her uncle at Twin-Star Labs, she acted as if we should be automatic best friends. I don't mean to sound cruel, but I preferred not to spend so much time with her. Suki was clingy and insecure, and she scared all the boys away with her mousey ways.

If she didn't stop hanging around me, I'd never fit in at Banbury High. At my old school in Salem, Oregon, I'd always been kind of an outsider.

I was branded a rebel in the second grade—all because of a misunderstanding on a rainy afternoon. The stigma stayed with me forever. Or at least until we moved to Banbury Bay.

Sometimes when I looked back on that strange day in Salem, I got goose bumps. I couldn't explain what happened, and all these years later I still wondered. *I don't want to think about that.* That is behind me now.

I saw our move to Banbury Bay as a chance to start a new life, with new friends. But I knew I couldn't spend every waking moment with Suki unless I wanted to be labeled a total spard. It's a hard, cold fact that the crowd you hang with influences how people view you.

"This old house of yours really gives me the creeps, Jenna," Suki said. "Your attic is probably full of rats. Let's get out of here!"

"No, I want to see what's in this old trunk," I said, pulling a rusty bicycle off the dust-coated trunk in the corner.

"Probably more spiders."

I ignored her and popped open the lid. A thick, musty odor nearly knocked me over.

"It's just a bunch of old clothes," she said, peering over my shoulder.

It didn't look like anything too exciting. They were mostly faded blue jeans and ragged T-shirts. But I dug through the pile, partly because I was hoping Suki would get tired of watching me and leave my house. "Look at this!" I said. "It's a pair of old overalls. Somebody embroidered little hearts and peace signs on them. Do you think they belonged to a farmer?"

"There's something sticking out of the pocket!"

It was an old diary. A *very* old diary—its secrets long ago locked between the fading red vinyl cover. It would be easy to pick the lock. Someone had scribbled PRIVATE across the cover. For an instant, I considered tucking it back in the overalls. After all, what right did I have to read a stranger's secrets?

"Who did it belong to?" Suki's pale blue eyes sparked with sudden interest.

"Whoever it was is probably dead," I said. *Do the dead have a right to privacy?* I wondered. I turned the little book over and set it on the floor. "I could pick the lock if I had a piece of wire." The words were barely out of my mouth when the lock suddenly popped open—all by itself.

"*Weird!*" Suki whispered. "Maybe you've got ghosts up here!"

A shiver ran through me, but I laughed it off. "Would you relax? The lock was just worn out. I must have jostled it when I set it down, and it broke. That's all."

I opened the diary and a black and white photograph fluttered out. I stared into the familiar face and gasped.

"That's you!" Suki said. "How did a picture of you get in that old diary? And who is that *cute* guy next to you?"

I couldn't answer her. All I could do was stare at the girl in the photograph. She had *my* face! The wide spaced eyes. The button nose sprinkled with freckles. The slight overbite and too thin lips. Those were *my* features. But it wasn't a picture of me. I was certain.

I turned over the photograph and read: *Rita and Ben, Stones concert, Seattle Coliseum, 1970.* That picture was a *hundred* years old!

I finally found my voice. "It's not me. This picture was taken a century ago."

"She sure looks like you. She's even built like you, Jenna."

It was true. Rita had my long (but too skinny) legs and slim waist. She wore a flowered halter top and a faded pair of cut-off jeans embroidered with peace signs. Had Rita embroidered the overalls too? They must have been hers, I realized.

"Maybe that's you in another life," Suki suggested. "Maybe you were reincarnated."

"She's probably a relative of mine. We have the same genes. It's natural I'd inherit some of my family's characteristics," I said, trying to make sense of the eerie resemblance.

"It's not like she's your mom or something for Pete's sake! She's a *distant* relative. If she was really born a hundred years ago, the genes would be watered down by now. You could inherit her nose or something, but not her *whole* face!"

Suki was right. It didn't make sense I would look so much like a relative who was born a century before me. The fact is, I don't even resemble anyone in my immediate family. My parents are both short and round, while I am long and slender. I don't have my dad's prominent nose or my mom's startling violet eyes. My nose is one of those tiny, upturned models and my eyes are an uninteresting gray. I'm different from my parents in so many ways, I can't even count them. I thought about this as I walked Suki home.

Her house is about a quarter of a mile from us. It's right on the water—so close the waves swish against her dining room window when it storms. When we arrived, Suki scurried inside and I leaned on the railing of the Gradys' deck and stared at the horizon. The sunset had deepened to purple, and the beach was cloaked in shadows. Suki's father, Dr. Grady, poked his head out the door. "It's getting dark. I'll drive you home," he said, his scraggly eyebrows drawing together in concern.

I waved him away. "I walk fast. I'll be home before it's completely dark. Tell Suki I'll phone her," I called over my shoulder.

I lied to Dr. Grady. I had no intention of walking fast. I strolled slowly, inhaling the pungent, salty air and savoring the peaceful moments alone. The only sound was the gentle slapping of the waves. It felt good to get away form Suki's constant chatter.

Halfway home, my finger-watch phone beeped. Suki's face—in 3-D—appeared on my watch face. *Now what does she want?*

"Jenna, are you there?" Suki called. "Can you hear me?"

For a moment, I felt as if a miniature Suki face was growing from my finger, like an annoying planter's wart that refused to fall off. I turned off the finger-phone and her image vanished. Then I settled in on one of the huge logs a storm had washed ashore and opened Rita's diary, which I had carried with me from home. The light had nearly faded away so I read by my keyring flashlight.

March 3, 1970

Dear Diary,

I never should have listened to April! She told me I should "Play hard to get!" She said Ben would lose interest if I didn't "Act aloof" once in a while. She said—AND I QUOTE—"Men like a little mystery."

Well, I took April's advice. And I'd give anything if I hadn't. While I was busy being aloof, some tramp got her claws into the love of my life!

Why did I listen to April? She's never even had a

boyfriend and has only been on three dates, and they were only with that skinny guy who bags groceries— Marvin Fudsomething-or-other. Does that make her an expert????? I think not!

Maybe April WANTED to break me and Ben up because Shane doesn't want to date her. (Shane Murdock is Ben's best friend and he's gorgeous—though not as gorgeous as Ben.)

I guess I shouldn't be mad at April, but I have to blame someone. It hurts so bad. For the first time in my life, I'm really in love. I know I've said it before, but it was NEVER like this. Oh, Diary, I know I haven't told you anything about Ben. And I know I promised to write my every thought in you. But I've been so busy since I met him, I haven't had time. Now, as my tears fall on your pages, smearing the ink, I'll try to fill you in on the last weeks.

Diary, it started with his eyes. Ben has these really far out eyes. They're the same shade of blue as a faded pair of jeans. And when he looks at me, I feel like he's looking into my soul. I know that sounds corny but—oh! Someone's knocking at the door. Maybe it's Ben!

I'm back, Diary. It wasn't Ben. No one was at the door. That's kind of scary, because I'm here alone. Mom's at her yoga class and Dad's giving a guitar lesson. Jim is probably out raising hell on his bicycle with all the other 11-year-old brats in the neighborhood. So when I answered the door and didn't see anybody, I slammed it fast. I kind of had the feeling someone was hiding in the bushes! I went around the house and locked all the windows, just in case. Lately I've had this really weird feeling that someone's watching me!

A sudden sharp crack interrupted Rita's words. I nearly dropped the diary as I turned quickly toward the noise. It sounded like a twig snapping under a foot. But I couldn't see anyone. Immersed in Rita's world, I hadn't noticed the night creep in. The logs were shapeless shadows blending with the beach, and the water had turned black.

"Who is it? Who's there?" I called out tentatively. "Suki, is that you?" It would be exactly like her to follow me home when I'd just gotten rid of her. The pest!

Only the waves answered me, their rhythmic whispers caressing the sand. I aimed my flashlight in the direction the noise had come from—or rather where it seemed to come from. On the water sound plays tricks. No one was there.

I stuffed the diary back into my pocket and headed toward home, this time walking briskly.

The distinct sound of footsteps crunching on rocks came behind me. *Someone is following me!*

My heartbeat thudded in my ears as I began to run. I bounded forward and my feet slid across the slippery, seaweed-coated rocks. Stumbling, I fell to my knees. Barnacles sharp as razors scraped the palms of my hands as I scrambled to my feet.

Adrenaline coursed through me, fueling me with a surge of energy that kept my legs pumping. I nearly flew over the beach, kicking unseen sticks and sea whips out of my path, running for my life.

I rounded the bend and was greeted by a ferocious bark. Relief flooded through me. It was old Mr. Edwards and his seeing-eye-dog, Jake.

"Who's there?" Mr. Edwards yelled.

I skidded to a stop, gasping for breath. "It's me, Mr. Edwards! It's Jenna. Someone was following me!"

"Don't worry. Jake will take care of them," he said. "You can walk with us. We wander down here every night so Jake can do his business. That way I don't have to clean up after him. The tide comes in and does it for me."

"Sounds like a good system," I said politely.

"May I give you a piece of advice, young lady?"

"Sure."

"Don't walk on the beach alone after dark anymore. It's not safe for you. Did you know a girl was murdered here?"